LIEUTENANT TOM PARIS FLEW LIKE HE WAS TRAPPED IN AN ASTEROID BELT . . .

Harry Kim sucked in his breath audibly while Paris dodged a couple of particularly nasty-looking bits of wreck, but the captain was so calm, she could have been playing 3-D chess in the *Voyager* lounge. Paris hit the acceleration hard across the paths of two major ships to avoid the debris and yanked down and hard port just as the dead weapons of an ancient warrior opened fire. . . .

Look for STAR TREK Fiction from Pocket Books

Star Trek: The Original Series

Star Trek: The Next Generation

Star Trek: Deep Space Nine

Star Trek: Voyager

CYBERSONG

S. N. Lewitt

POCKET BOOKS

New York London Toronto Sydney Tokyo Singapore

An *Original* Publication of POCKET BOOKS

POCKET BOOKS, a division of Simon & Schuster Inc.
1230 Avenue of the Americas, New York, NY 10020

ISBN: 0-671-56783-7

First Pocket Books printing June 1996

10 9 8 7 6 5 4 3 2

CYBERSONG

CHAPTER

1

SHE WAS LONELY AND AFRAID. THAT HAD BEEN AS BAD as the thirst. The Kazon-Ogla weren't generous with their captives, and their water was their wealth. They didn't waste it on captive labor. Once the lot was used up and dead, there would be plenty of others.

Being afraid wasn't good, but she understood that fear didn't mean she didn't have courage as well. Fear was a warning sign. There was no shame to it. It was how she acted that mattered, not how scared she was.

Here in the prison camp, there was nothing but fear. She curled on her bunk, if the thin dusty blanket over a pile of rags could be called that. The rags were clothes other slave laborers had died wearing. Her own gray tunic was stiff with sweat and old blood. At least she couldn't smell it anymore. After weeks of captivity she had become inured to the stench of death and excrement in what passed as shelter for the labor gang.

No, the loneliness was worst of all. That there were no others like her was bad enough. No one who remembered the ordered courtyards of the Ocampa. Not one of the other prisoners was of her race. But worse, not one of the other prisoners cared about anything beyond themselves—their next drink, their hope for escape.

She thought that they must have been different before captivity. The grinding drudgery of the mines and the unrelenting thirst would drive even the best person to selfish madness after a time. She reminded herself of how close she had come to mindless hatred from weariness and anger, how the thirst had driven her more than any idea had inspired her.

That was what she had feared more than she had feared death, or the mines, or the next morning as a slave of the Kazon. The capacity for evil was inside her. It was inside everyone. She knew it, she had felt and tasted it every time she entered the mines.

That fear made her lonely. She couldn't talk to anyone, couldn't share a memory or a song. Nothing mattered when she was so terribly, frightfully alone. She wasn't even sure she existed anymore . . .

Kes awoke trembling, clutching a soft blanket around her. It was thick and warm and smelled of soft purfume, telling her that she was safe. She hadn't had nightmares in a long time. Immediately she patted the space beside her, and it was empty. Neelix was gone, then, probably preparing breakfast.

Neelix's absence explained the dream she told herself firmly. She was never alone on *Voyager*. Neelix was always there, or The Doctor, or a patient, or someone who needed her help. And she was glad that she could help, that she was part of the crew.

She had overslept, she realized. Last night she had stayed late after dinner studying respiratory systems with The Doctor. The differences between humans and Vulcans and Talaxians were so fascinating that they had completely lost track of time. Kes never would have come to sleep at all if Neelix hadn't found her in sickbay looking at holograms of various types of lungs and oxygen exchanges.

"Of course, we're only looking at the oxygen-breathing species now," The Doctor had said. "In the Alpha Quadrant we know of species that breathe methane and chlorine as well, though they are less common than oxygen breathers."

"I have heard of a race that breathes poison air," Kes had replied. "Do you have diagrams for these other lung systems as well?"

"Of course," The Doctor told her. "But, it's a completely different biochemistry, and the best way to approach it would be from a chemical level before looking at gross anatomy."

"The best approach is to get a good night's sleep," Neelix said, coming in to claim Kes from her studies. "Do you have any idea how late it is? I've been searching all over the ship for you. I thought something might have happened."

Kes had stood and smiled at him. "It is late. I hadn't realized I was so tired. Doctor, could we continue this tomorrow?"

"If we don't have six more sprained ankles and wrists from that holodeck adventure," The Doctor said.

Kes laughed softly as Neelix propelled her out of sickbay.

"What was that about?" the Talaxian asked sharply. "Has someone been trying to get you to go off to the holodeck alone?"

Kes shook her head. "After the injuries I've seen, I wouldn't be interested in trying out this new program, no matter how much everyone seems to enjoy it. Though when Tom Paris told me what skiing was like, it did sound like a dream. No wonder everyone is going."

"And when did Mr. Paris talk to you about this new holodeck skiing?" Neelix asked, his tone tinged with suspicion.

"When The Doctor was taping up his ankle," Kes replied evenly. "He was one of the first injuries. And he complained the whole time because we weren't using any of the more sophisticated techniques to repair all the damage. The Doctor

4

thought if they had to feel it a while, they would be more careful."

Neelix only snorted. Kes sighed and started toward her quarters. "I'm tired. I've been fixing minor injuries all day and studying half the evening. I don't even remember having dinner." Her voice was gentle. Neelix followed her to the turbo-lift.

She remembered going to sleep immediately, and then there was the dream. The dream was more real than the conversation about the skiing program, more real than anything she had encountered on the holodeck.

Voyager itself was enough of a fantasy for her. Being rescued from the Kazon would have been enough. To live free among the stars, to have the luxuries of learning and friendship aboard *Voyager*, was far more than Kes had ever dreamed.

She thought of all these things as she got washed. She thought of the good friends she had made here, the kind and warm people who had become her world.

And still she couldn't shake off the fear and loneliness from the dream. No matter how firmly she told herself that it was nothing, she couldn't rinse away the lingering shreds of anxiety and isolation with soap.

No, she thought as she put on her rust-colored tunic, she would talk to The Doctor about this. He had been programmed with the entire history of psychological inquiry. He had access to the records of Betazoid healers who understood empathic gifts. Though Kes had never really defined her knowing as empathy.

She combed her short blond hair quickly and turned from the mirror. She wasn't immediately hungry, but if the nightmare had come from skipping dinner, then she knew she should eat something. Neelix had put a bowl of Iobrian bluefruit on the main table. Kes picked one up and nibbled at it as she considered further.

While The Doctor might have the information to test her and even train her, she was not Betazoid. There was no reason to assume that their methods would be useful to Kes, or even applicable. And besides, Kes had no desire to interrupt her obviously necessary and endlessly fascinating medical studies for something that might be of limited value.

But she could still tell The Doctor everything, and perhaps one of them could determine whether it was just a particularly bad nightmare she had had, or whether it was something more.

CHAPTER

2

"CAPTAIN, TACHYON DENSITY IN THIS REGION IS TWO point three times normal," Ensign Harry Kim said. He had just reported to his station and run his normal check-in routine.

"Check the log, Mr. Kim," Captain Janeway ordered. "How long have we noted elevated levels?"

He queried the night's logs and studied the readout for a moment before answering. "It's been a steady rise since approximately zero two hundred hours. Slow, but increasing regularly. If this keeps up, it's going to interfere with ship's systems in another four hours."

Captain Kathryn Janeway sat forward and stared at the screen. Space before them was black and empty. The few distant stars shone dull at the edges of the display and were the only indication that the viewer was functioning at all.

"Plot the vector of the tachyon density and see if it's emanating from any object in this area, Mr. Kim," the captain ordered. "And check for debris. This could just be the signature of an old event that shouldn't be a problem. If you find something, let's take a look at it."

"Yes, Captain," the young officer replied, and immediately bent his head over his console once more. "There's something out there, but the heavy tachyon concentration is making it hard to get a decent image."

The large viewscreen on the bridge stuttered with static. Between bursts of gray interference, the vague likeness of several ships appeared. They were exotic in form, and the few that could be seen together looked different from each other as well. Even though Janeway had seen all manner of spacecraft from myriad races, she was hard-pressed to identify the hulks that flickered in the badly resolved picture. The torn fragments mostly showed the regular curves of formed materials. And from the dull glow where the light hit them, it appeared that most of the pieces were refined metals.

"There seems to be some kind of communications band emanating from that source," Lieutenant Tuvok, the Vulcan security officer said. "But I cannot get it to resolve."

"I could try filtering out some of the heavy tachyon interference," Harry Kim offered.

"Thank you, Mr. Kim," the Vulcan replied. "However, I have already attempted that and have made the adjustments necessary to boost the signal as well. I cannot get anything . . . We've lost it."

"Have they stopped transmitting?" Lieutenant Paris asked.

"If I knew that the transmission had stopped, or been interrupted, I would have indicated that information," the Vulcan said dispassionately. "In fact, what we did manage to intercept was data-dense computer relay protocols."

"So they're more interested in talking to our computer than talking to us," Tom Paris noted aloud. "Sound like real hospitable folk."

Harry Kim shook his head slightly at Paris's comment. They were good enough friends that no more was needed to remind them both of their encounter with the Sikarians, the most hospitable folk in the Delta Quadrant. The people who had technology to help them get at least a good way closer to home had downright refused. The word "hospitable" had had a double-edged meaning aboard *Voyager* ever since.

"Shall we investigate further, Captain?" the Vulcan asked.

Captain Janeway watched the display screen. Her wary eyes remained calm and her mouth set firm, giving away nothing. She remained silent for a moment, considering her options. She had insisted that *Voyager* fulfill all of Starfleet's objectives, even though the ship was farther from Federation space than any starship had ever been; that included scientific investigation and contact with new races.

But that objective didn't require her to study everything in the Delta Quadrant. There were plenty of planets and peoples here they couldn't avoid, restocking stops that had to be made on the long journey home. They didn't need to go poking around what appeared to be a junk heap, not unless there was some very good reason to think that it would help them get home.

"It does not have any of the characteristics of the Array or the Caretaker," Mr. Tuvok said. "There is no indication that this is anything more than a garbage dump."

The captain smiled slightly. "I don't believe we need a detour," she said. "Steady as she goes, Mr. Paris."

There was an air of calm on the bridge. The monitors glowed amber, red, green, and blue, turning palms into brilliant array as skilled hands hovered over control panels. The hush of concentration was reinforced by the silence from the screen. Janeway stared into the darkness displayed before them.

The captain didn't say that there was no place to stop for provisions for a very long time. She was worried about stores. Without the replicators working at full capacity, there was a chance that they would be running low on food before they found the next planet where they could stop for supplies.

There was no reason for the crew to know about the potential shortage in too much detail. Everyone knew that food and power couldn't be wasted. That was enough.

She only hoped that the information Neelix had provided was correct. He hadn't wanted to come this way in the first place. But the other routes were much longer and not reliably stocked, either.

"I've never been there myself," he had told her when they had discussed the route. "But this planet is inhabited and their people are spacefaring. Not much, you understand. They're generally known to be rather insular, and their religion is very demanding. You can't ever tell when they'll be in the mood to trade, but I know they're there and that they grow crops of things we can eat."

"Sounds like a better alternative than the others," Janeway had replied. She hadn't really liked any of the choices available. But this sector of the Delta Quadrant was one of the "bubbles" in space, a fairly large area with few stars.

"Let's take a look at that computer transmission," Janeway ordered. "If it's anything interesting, we could look further. But without more data, we can ignore this."

Now she was curious, but even with communication from somewhere in here, she disliked this empty sector. And she didn't want to linger here. Not while their food supply was running low and there was nothing at all for weeks away.

"Computer, give the text of latest transmission," the captain said in an even voice.

"There was no text in that transmission," the computer's mechanical voice replied.

Janeway shook her head slightly. Computers could be maddeningly literal and needed to be prodded every step of the way. Janeway carefully kept the frustration out of her voice as she queried for further information.

Frustration at the computer was as useless as frustration at their situation.

She remembered a leadership course at the Academy where the psychologists in charge had instructed the cadets to use their anger, to turn that energy into something productive.

Kathryn Janeway did not agree, not anymore. That was useful for planetside problems that hard work and determination could solve. Those psychologists had never been stuck on the other side of the galaxy, responsible for a crew torn from their families, their lives, from all humanity they had known or expected to know.

"Dataset includes target coordinates," the computer said emotionlessly. *"Voyager* is instructed to arrive at zero point seven three vector six, warp three."

"That's the middle of that thing," Tom Paris said.

"Computer, is there any further information?" the captain asked.

"Additional data is not available," the computer voice replied.

"Then we have no reason to suspect going here will do anything but waste time," Janeway said. She didn't add the phrase "and resources," though she couldn't avoid the thought. "Mr. Paris, ignore the computer coordinates and remain on course." She touched her commbadge and spoke quietly. "Mr. Neelix, meet me in my ready room." Then the captain left the bridge.

When Neelix arrived in the ready room, Captain Janeway was staring at an inventory list. She didn't switch off the display when the Talaxian arrived, dressed in his usual brightly colored motley attire that clashed with the restful tones around him. He sat in one of the high-back upholstered chairs and waited until the captain was ready to acknowledge him.

"Mr. Neelix, I have a question for you about this region. However, before we begin I would like you to look at this listing from stores. According to this morning's tally, we have less than half the Grolian flour and pineapples left. Our estimates last month were for us to have at least seventy percent of those items remaining before we entered this zone."

Neelix stared at the figures displayed before him and shook his head. "I don't know, Captain. I was certain we had more than that."

"You didn't move any to a place the provisions officer wouldn't find it?" Janeway asked. "You didn't take supplies down to your galley, or maybe put them elsewhere?"

The Talaxian shook his head. "No, Captain. There was some mold in the flour. I put it in the freezer where it would be killed. And I threw out the molded bags. But freezing generally keeps the rest from going bad."

"And the apples?" Janeway asked, refusing to react until she had a complete report.

"Oh, the apples were used," Neelix said, rubbing his hands. "My apple pie last week. Everyone loved it. They talked about it for days. Why even yesterday Mr. Kim asked me if I was going to make more."

The captain stared coolly at the cook. "Those apples have exceptional longevity, or so you told me. We don't have the luxury of desserts using up provisions that we could well need before we can replenish our supplies. And in the case of the tainted grain, you have to inform me and the provisions officer immediately. I can't make good decisions with bad information."

Neelix rose and pulled himself to his full inconsiderable height. "Captain, as this ship's morale officer, I decided that desserts are an important part of our diet and routine. I do not make extravagant meals all the time, but after something traumatic, well, the crew needs a pick-me-up. And we'll get to Tsrana in less than three weeks. As long as the Tsranans are willing to trade, we won't have any trouble at all."

"As long as the Tsranans are willing to trade?" Janeway asked, her hopes sinking.

"Oh, I'm sure we can work something out, as long as it isn't one of their closed days."

Captain Janeway sighed. Closed days. She had heard of cultures in the Alpha Quadrant like this, semi-isolationists who wanted the goods trade brought but didn't want to interact with aliens. They were never easy to get along with, and trade was always troublesome at best.

"Don't give it a second thought, Captain. I know a great deal about the Tsranans. I'm sure we can arrange a very reasonable trade," Neelix tried to reassure her.

There were times when the Talaxian deeply tried Captain Janeway's patience. He said he knew this sector, but much of his knowledge was based on hearsay and rumor, and often his estimates were more optimistic than pragmatic.

"If we get to Tsrana on time, we'll still be cutting it close," Janeway said. "We don't have any reserves in case of a delay or an emergency, and as it is, we're going to be down to Meezian stew for the last three days as it is."

"I make wonderful Meezian stew," Neelix said, rubbing his hands together. "And it's very nutritious."

"That's not the point, Mr. Neelix," the captain said crisply. "The point is, we are very low on supplies, and it's a long way until we get provisions. So I want to see some real economy in our use of what we have. Do you understand?"

"Will that be all?" Neelix asked. "I have to go start the vegetables for dinner. We're having a new creation. Mr. Paris told me about pot pies, and while I don't have a recipe or the traditional ingredients he mentioned, I think I have an idea to make it even better."

It took all of the captain's training, experience, and natural reserve not to wince. What Neelix did to native Earth dishes was best left unimagined, not to mention what he did to *plomeek* soup.

"There is something else," the captain said. "Please sit back down. You told me when we discussed courses several weeks ago that there was some danger in the region, but you never specified what it was. I would like to hear it, and I would like to know how you know."

Neelix cleared his throat and stroked the dark glass of the table before him. "Well, Captain, everyone knows there is something lurking here that lures in ships and leaves them. It's an old story. My grandmother told me when her grandfather was on a ship that passed close to the Singing Quarter they took on a passenger who had escaped from the trap. The singing is the trap, the passenger said. I don't know what that means, precisely, but a lot of ships have been lost, never traced and never found. Like a black hole swallowed them up."

"Our readings show no indication of any black

holes for light years in any direction," Janeway said, musing. "But those hulks out there in the tachyon field . . . Computer, display the image we picked up of the transmitting ship."

As the computer promptly recreated the picture on the small personal screen in the ready room, Janeway told Neelix to look at it. "Is there anything here you can identify?" she asked as Neelix studied the remains of spacecraft displayed before him.

"That one," he said, jabbing his finger at an indistinct object in the array.

"Full magnification," the captain ordered.

What had been little more than a vague shadow filled the screen with detail. Red marks, presumably writing, marched down one side of the craft to where it had been ripped open. A few small tendrils of dead wire drifted out the open lock.

Neelix trembled.

"Mr. Neelix, you look like you've seen a ghost," the captain said.

"Yes, Captain," Neelix replied. "I have."

CHAPTER
3

"MR. PARIS, CHECK YOUR HEADINGS," COMMANDER Chakotay, the first officer said. "The captain said that we are not investigating this phenomena."

"Yes, sir," Tom Paris replied. "I've been keeping us on a steady course, headed around the tachyon cloud."

"I suggest that you check that again," Chakotay said dryly.

Paris ran his fingers over his instruments as if he didn't have to watch to know exactly what he would find.

"No, sir, according to all my readouts, there is no course deviation."

Chakotay stared at the main screen without seeing the display. He didn't really trust Paris, and he didn't have any choice but to trust him. Every day on *Voyager* he had to rely on a man who had betrayed him.

For some people this would be impossible. For Chakotay it was merely difficult. And he had done far more difficult things before.

Right now was not one of those times. Right now Chakotay knew that something was wrong. Something subtle and slippery, something that he couldn't immediately identify.

He knew they weren't on the right course. Everything looked right. The forward display was mostly dark broken by a few steady stars in the distance and glints off objects that looked like space junk—random rocks or bits of water vapor that froze in absolute zero to become beautiful reflectors. Nothing appeared out of the ordinary at all.

But Paris wasn't lying. The computer gave out data that confirmed their current course. The screen before him showed empty space with just a few distant stars. There was no reason for him to suspect a problem—except for the intuition that he had trusted all his life, the sixth sense that had rarely been wrong before.

He had no evidence to bring to the captain, who was busy in conference with Neelix. But he knew he had to do something, and soon, before irreparable damage was done.

He knew that even a small alteration of course could destroy them. The captain had not shared her concern about supplies with him, but that didn't mean he wasn't aware of both the problem and her doubt. He had seen enough of the stores and the calculations over this part of the journey to know that the two matched far too closely for comfort. Chakotay rose warily from the captain's chair and moved toward Ensign Kim's station. Harry did not notice the commander's approach. His fingers danced across the board and his eyes remained fixed on the monitor.

"Mr. Kim, how are those tachyon readings? Is the bombardment still high, or have we already passed into a lower range?" he asked, careful to keep his voice controlled as if he merely wanted additional data.

The young ensign looked up, startled. He studied his board once more and his face became tense. "That's odd," he said, and checked again before making a formal report. "The tachyon bombardment has increased, even though we should be pulling away from the cloud."

The commander nodded. "Mr. Paris, according to your readings, should we have emerged from the bombardment by now?"

But before the question was out of Chakotay's mouth, Tom Paris was shaking his head vigorously in response. "No, this is just wrong," Paris said.

Chakotay strode toward the helmsman's station, put his hand on the back of the chair, and looked over Paris' shoulder. *At least there should be some drop in the readings. Certainly it shouldn't have gotten worse,* Chakotay thought as Paris' monitor beeped at him mockingly.

"We should have passed out of the field six minutes ago," Paris reported. "There is still tachyon activity at the edges of the cloud, but it doesn't make any sense for it to be increasing, sir."

"No," Chakotay agreed. "It doesn't make sense." The executive officer felt a chill. Janeway was still closeted with their Talaxian guide. He could call her, but he decided to test further.

If they lost half an hour, he would take the responsibility. Captain Janeway expected her officers to be able to act independently, to make decisions. She relied on him most of all for this quality. After all, he had been a commanding officer himself once, and not so long ago. Command was not an easy habit to acquire, but once learned it was never entirely laid aside.

"As an experiment, Mr. Paris, take us about to mark seven point zero two three. And Mr. Kim, watch those tachyon readings and report any change immediately."

The entire staff on the bridge looked at him. Only the Vulcan security officer nodded once, signaling his comprehension of the tactic. The others merely turned to their work.

"Ready to bring her about on mark seven point zero two three, warp three. Now," Tom Paris said, indicating the course change.

The bridge was silent. Everyone waited, eyes on

Harry Kim. The young ensign said nothing, his eyes glued to his console, his mouth frowning with tension.

Chakotay waited. Ten minutes, he decided. He would wait that long. In ten minutes at warp three they should be well gone. In ten seconds at warp three there should be changes, he knew. And as the silence grew he knew there was something very wrong indeed.

Ten minutes? He cut it in half. Five. There had to be some change. Something. Maybe he hadn't been entirely clear. The minutes moved slowly. His breathing sounded loud and harsh.

"Mr. Kim?" he asked over half a minute early.

"No change, sir," the helmsman replied promptly. "Maybe getting a little heavier, but with this much interference it's difficult to calibrate as precisely as we might like.

"What does it mean, sir?" Tom Paris asked.

Chakotay never took his eyes from the screen in front of them. "It means that something is very wrong, Mr. Paris."

"It was a long time ago when I was still in school," Neelix was telling the captain. "My brother was working on a merchant vessel before the war with Hace Konia broke out. And one school break I went with him on a short hop to learn a little, but mostly because he thought it would be good for me to get me away from our parents. They were very protective. Maybe he was right and they were

22

overprotective. But they were stricter with him than with me. He wasn't allowed to go camping until he was twelve." Neelix drew a breath and looked at the pictures up on the bulkhead of the ready room. He studied one and then moved on restlessly, flicking a hand in the air as if to whisk away an imaginary insect.

"Anyway, that doesn't really matter. What does is this. I was aboard the freighter, and I saw it with my own eyes. A single Rhiellian was drifting in space in his capsule, and he was still alive. We picked him up, but he was a typical Rhiellian; he protested and blamed us for saving his life. The rest of his corda were gone, and he didn't know what had happened. They had received a distorted distress call and had gone into an active tachyon cloud. From there his description was distorted. All he could talk about was loneliness, how horrible and cold the dark was.

"That part is about being Rhiellian, of course. He had lost his corda. Maybe we should have let him die. They can't exist without their group minds, and his own people would put him to death. It's shameful for them to be left alone, to have survived their entire hive."

Janeway raised her eyebrows quizzically.

"Their cordas are group minds linked up somehow with an AI."

"Like the Borg?" Janeway asked, her attention riveted.

"Borg?" Neelix asked.

"They're also a linked group mind with an AI," the captain said. "We've been at war. They want to assimilate all the sentient races they find, bring them into their mental collective. We think the Borg came from the Delta Quadrant. Be thankful you haven't encountered them yet."

"Oh no," Neelix said quickly. "The Rhiellians are very peaceable. I've never heard of them ever being in a war. No, they stay to themselves and don't bother anyone. So finding any of them in space is unusual to start. They don't have many trading ships. If you want their products, you go to them. And finding one alone—well, no one's ever found a Rhiellian alone."

Neelix sighed heavily. "That's all I know, Captain. Except that obviously something terrible happened, and the vector and the tachyon field readings match. But precisely what, well, no one can say.

"The Rhiellian talked about old gods and being seduced and music and all kinds of things that didn't make sense. But without the rest of the corda, no one expects a Rhiellian to make sense anyway."

They sat for a moment. Janeway didn't like having to rely on Neelix for information. It was worse when his knowledge came from some painful experience. She wouldn't have had to dredge personal memories back in the Alpha Quadrant, where every race was well documented and all she had to do was access the computer files. Even large

parts of the Gamma Quadrant were getting familiar due to the wormhole.

Here she had no choice. Much as she would
prefer to leave Neelix's personal life untouched,
she knew that his information was necessary.

"Sounds like a good place to avoid," she agreed.
"Thank you, Neelix."

"Lunch will be a little late, Captain," he warned
her as he left. "I had a lot of chopping to do and
now it's going to be behind schedule. But I'm using
the rest of the Grolian flour to make cookies. No
more fancy desserts, just cookies. Mr. Kim's Cookies. I love it when the sounds go so well, and they
were his idea. That way people can take their
desserts with them."

She smiled as the door closed behind him. There
was something likable in the way he took to the role
he had created. As if cooking were on the same
level as engineering.

Janeway left the calm retreat of her ready room,
decorated with relics of her scientific past, to return
to the bridge of her ship. Chakotay's face was
drawn and tense as she strode to her place.

"Captain, we have a problem," Chakotay told
her. "The navigational readings say we are headed
around the tachyon field, but the tachyon readings
have increased dramatically. And the increase is
consistent even when we change headings."

"Have you checked the navigational systems and
the console connections?" the captain asked. Her
eyes flickered over the forward screen, the consoles

under control, and all the monitors she could sweep with a single turn of her head.

"We've checked out everything we could think of and the readings remain consistent," Chakotay told her.

Kathryn Janeway took her central seat on the bridge and leaned back, aware that all eyes were on her. She studied her own personal readout discreetly nestled deep in the arm of the command chair before she spoke. "Cut all engines," she said.

"All power cut," Paris replied, his voice tinged with surprise.

The captain smiled. "If we don't know which way we're going, it's better to stay put than to run at full speed in the wrong direction. Reverse impulse."

She waited until Paris announced, "We're coming to full stop," before she spoke again.

"What is the tachyon field reading now?" Janeway asked.

"Still increasing, Captain," Harry Kim replied, the surprise evident in his tone.

Janeway touched her commbadge. "Janeway to Engineering. B'Elanna, what's going on down there? Are we still generating warp speed?"

"Yes, Captain," Torres's voice sounded firm and a little confused. "Everything is on line and we're at warp six as ordered."

"I just ordered our speed cut," the captain replied.

"I'll check the connection, Captain," Torres replied, "but there wasn't any warning that there had been a change in course or speed. And that system shouldn't be out." The entire bridge could hear the chief engineer fuming at her boards as if they had somehow defied her on purpose.

"Get the warp drive off line and slow us to impulse," the captain ordered the engineer. "Then get up here immediately. And bring the engineering log for the past hour."

Few things made Kathryn Janeway really angry. But a threat to her ship or to her crew was a personal affront. And whatever was going on here was trying to wrest the ship from her command, and that was something she would not tolerate.

She stared out into the void depicted on the forward screen as if she could sight her enemy. "Not my ship, you don't," she muttered under her breath.

"Captain," B'Elanna Torres's voice came over the comm. "I've tried to cut the drive, but the warp coil isn't responding to the controls. I tried the override and everything behaves as if the boards are disconnected. We're checking the connection now, Captain, but it doesn't make sense that every station in Engineering is out."

"I'm on my way down," the captain replied. "Chakotay, take the bridge. Mr. Tuvok, come with me."

The security officer dropped in behind her and

said nothing until they were in the turbolift. "Why did you require my presence in Engineering?" the Vulcan asked.

"Because, Mr. Tuvok, this doesn't look like something natural to me," the captain replied. "This is starting to look very ugly. And I can't rule out sabotage."

CHAPTER 4

"KES, I TOLD YOU TWO CC'S OF THE ARELETHYNE, NOT the tridonal. Now this will all have to be done over again," The Doctor fumed.

Kes looked down and apologized. She studied the magnified display of the genetic material they were culturing and comparing. The intricate linked rings that appeared on the screen were meaningless to her, though she knew that she ought to know what they meant. She just was too distracted, and the experiment didn't feel important enough to command her full attention. Maybe she would concentrate better if there were some minor injuries from that holodeck program, or a couple of mashed fingers from the gym.

"It's just a good thing we don't have any patients

here now," the hologram continued. "This isn't like you at all. You're usually very efficient."

Kes thought about that. Usually dreams, even nightmares, stayed at home. By the time she was into a day's work, any shred of the night was gone.

This time it was different. She felt lonelier and more afraid as the hours passed, as if the dream had somehow settled into her waking life.

Its effect on her work was embarrassing. She was proud of what she was learning with The Doctor, pleased to make a valuable contribution to the ship that had become her life. She had never felt herself to be particularly valuable before, and there was deep pleasure in being able to do something important.

"Remember, I am programmed with as much psychoanalytic data as physical therapy," The Doctor told her.

Kes sighed. "It's just that I had a very bad dream, and I can't seem to shake it off," she said simply.

"A dream?" The Doctor asked, interest filling his face. "Dreams can be important." He sat at his desk chair and gestured to Kes to sit across from him. She took his suggestion readily, turning from the experiment and data as if it weren't even there.

Kes smiled. "I don't think so, really. This was just about being a prisoner in the mines, and being so lonely and afraid. And even though I know I'm here on *Voyager* now, I'm still aware of the feelings. I can't decide whether it's from the dream or from memory. Though dwelling on that memory isn't very helpful," she admitted. She got up and turned toward the work they had been doing as if she wanted to check the status. Her narrow fingers brushed the experimental containment fields that would have to be started all over again.

"I don't have any information on the typical dream life of the Ocampa," The Doctor admitted. "But every intelligent species has considered dreaming important. Among humans it's often considered to indicate a psychological state and condition. Chakotay's people think that some dreams are messages from the spirit realms. And among the Betazoids, dreams with powerful emotional content are often markers of empathic episodes, though given a familiar form by the dreamer who doesn't know that the underlying emotions of the dream began elsewhere. Do any of these sound applicable?"

Kes hesitated, considering the possibilities The Doctor had outlined. "I don't know," she finally admitted. "But it is still hard for me to think about that time, to remember it all."

"That's normal," The Doctor reassured her perfunctorily. "Trauma is often forgotten, at least in part. It's a survival mechanism."

"Yes, I suppose it would be," Kes answered.

"Perhaps it's time for you to remember now, now that you are in a safe environment," The Doctor said, his tone interested.

The Doctor may well be right though, she acknowledged. She had never been so secure, so valued, in all her life. And so many of her memories were a blur. Even her rebellion before she had left her people was not really clear.

She could remember her parents just a little, and a few days of schooling. There must have been more. She remembered Lezen sitting in the square telling them that there was a time before the Caretaker, when the Ocampa were free people who had lived above the surface.

She tried to remember meeting Neelix. He had rescued her, and she had known him then. But she couldn't remember what it was, or why Neelix had been in the mine before.

She couldn't picture her Ocampa clothes; she couldn't even recall what color they were. And yet she knew the colors of everything she wore now, the violet and peach and pink dresses, the soft complex colors that she loved.

All she could recall plainly was the mine, the driving thirst and the grit in her throat. The chalky taste of dried rations and the red sand that got into every crevasse, every pore, that she thought she would never be able to scrub clean. She remembered this all so clearly it was more real than The Doctor sitting before her.

And then she held up one hand to her eyes. Was it reality she remembered so very clearly, or was it the dream?

Finally, Kes took her hand down and turned her

eyes back to The Doctor. He was a hologram, she knew that. But he was also her friend and her mentor, and he was as fully a person as herself. She trusted him.

"Do you have an idea of how to recover my memory?" Kes asked quietly.

"There are several methods used by different schools of theory," The Doctor said. "Hypnosis is always popular, the idea being that the individual never forgets anything, only represses it. There is talk therapy, discussing different aspects until things start to make sense. That can take a long time. And then there's reenactment, where the patient confronts the realities of the past and acts them out again, but this time changes things to effect the outcome. Taking charge of the past and rewriting it."

"I don't know that there's anything to rewrite," Kes said quietly. "But how is this reenactment done?"

"Well, we could certainly do it on the holodeck," The Doctor said. "You would have to create the program, and then you go and live it out."

"I don't know how to make a holodeck program," Kes said. "I haven't been on the holodeck much, except for a picnic with Neelix. He wouldn't like me going with anyone else."

"Well, I'm sure someone would help you with the program," The Doctor said. "All you would have to do is to describe your memories to the best of your ability. Then as you reenact it, you can change things as you remember, to make them more realistic."

"I would like you to come with me," Kes said.

"What?" The Doctor asked. He blinked. He had gone to the holodeck before. In fact, it was one of the few places outside of sickbay he could go and retain his full integrity. After all, the holodeck was set up for holograms.

"Why?" he asked, bemused.

"To explain it as we go along," Kes said. "Isn't it true that you're not supposed to try therapeutic techniques alone?"

The Doctor was silent. He couldn't refute her, not when he himself remembered saying that to her in one of their very few discussions of psychotherapy.

"Well, of course a patient isn't supposed to be alone throughout the process. But breakthroughs happen all the time, not just during the therapeutic hour. That time is reserved to reflect and understand new insights."

Kes smiled softly. "And do you believe that, Doctor? Or do you just want more encouragement to return to the holodeck?"

"It might be nice to get out of sickbay," he grudgingly replied. "But where you're going isn't where I would choose."

"And what would you choose?"

The Doctor cocked his head to one side. He had to think for a moment. "There are a lot of places and times before direct download was possible. Galen, Hippocrates—it would be interesting to talk to Hippocrates. But if I had to choose only one, I think it would be Louis Pasteur. You remember who he was?"

The question was rhetorical. Kes never forgot anything. "The first human to create a vaccine," she answered promptly.

"Preventing disease is better than curing it," The Doctor acknowledged. "Not that we'll have any time for any research here." He sighed at the remains of the ruined experiment. Kes turned away and hung her head.

"Not as long as they keep playing with that ski program," Kes agreed.

Then Kes and The Doctor both smiled together. Kes knew they were thinking the same thing. If she took over the holodeck for her therapy, it would cut down on ski injuries for the day.

He was sitting in the captain's chair on the bridge. Chakotay knew that. And he was concentrating firmly on the problem at hand. Still, his thoughts kept wandering in a way he had trained against for years, ever since he had been a youngster.

Maybe it was just indigestion, he thought. He had sampled several of Neelix's cookies after dinner. In truth, dinner had been too unpalatable to eat, but he had still been hungry. The cookies hadn't been bad, which had been a surprise. They were probably the first thing Neelix had ever created that Chakotay could actually say that he liked. And he had eaten a good number of them.

And now he felt—unquiet. As if everything were slightly askew. Like the forest before a great storm when the birds became still. There was nothing here he could identify as wrong, but it didn't really seem right, either.

There was something else, the taste of loneliness, the fear and the isolation he hadn't experienced until he had gone to Starfleet Academy. During all the time he had had to be alone during his training before he left for the Academy, there was always a feeling of connection. He had been part of the world, of the many animal spirits that walked and flew and crawled around him. There were the tree spirits and the great mountains.

When he had gone to the Academy, he had left all of that behind and he had been miserable. The academic program had taken up every moment of his waking life and then some.

He thought he had been disciplined when he arrived at the Academy, but he had learned differently. There he found a new kind of discipline of spirit, an ability to do more, work harder, and stay up longer than he had ever imagined existed.

But the loneliness and being cut off from the spirit world had been terrible. He had felt as if there were an invisible barrier between him and all the other cadets, that he couldn't touch their souls.

There were no animals, nothing from the natural

world he loved, in the Academy. And so he had been terribly, wrenchingly lonely.

But this wasn't the place to be remembering those things, he realized with a wrench. That was long past, and now he had duties and responsibilities . . . And his carefully disciplined mind was drifting off as if he were drugged.

Chakotay gripped the arms of the captain's chair and shook himself slightly. He tried to concentrate on the familiar sights and noises of the bridge, the endless starfield on the screen, the soft padding of crew members' feet as they walked behind him doing their work, the comforting beeps of the consoles. Yet Chakotay still felt disconnected from the rest of the crew on the bridge, even those in the meeting with the captain. Some of them were people he had served with for years, people he considered close friends.

From here he could see Paris bent over the helm, and Ensign Mkubata at the nav where often Harry Kim was assigned. Kim was in conference with the captain now, adding his expertise where it would be most useful. Chakotay remembered the last game of pool he had played with Harry in Paris's re-creation of a French bar on the holodeck. He could even smell the brandy if he thought about it, feel the smooth wood of the cue in his hand.

It did no good. The loneliness was there, assaulting him.

He tried to unravel it, and somehow fact stood against the unflagging misery that had caught him.

He had not been lonely at the Academy, he remembered with a start. There had been the entire lacrosse team and his roomates, Gregor Marchenko and Tony Long. But Gregor had been killed in the rescue mission to the Andorian colonies . . . and with that thought, the loneliness hit harder than ever.

Chakotay made a decision. He was going to ignore it. He was going to work. He had done this before.

Only he had never felt so lonely before. Never.

CHAPTER

5

"Sabotage?" B'Elanna Torres asked, immediately looking to the sides as if to check an enemy approach. All she could see were the few officers in the captain's ready room. Harry Kim was on her left, studying the graphic display in the monitor over her shoulder and comparing it to his own.

"The log clearly shows that the correct instructions were read into the system," Tuvok said. "This is not an instance of anyone on the bridge or down in Engineering making a mistake." Or the kind of strange intrusion they had encountered before, when an alien creature had taken over Tuvok himself. Everyone delicately refrained from reminding him.

"If the log is correct, there is a massive malfunction in the computer system," the Vulcan continued.

"I started a level three diagnostic," Torres interjected. "It takes a couple of hours to run, but at least we'll know if the system's at fault."

"Two point five nine hours, to be exact," Tuvok corrected her. "If there is no computer malfunction, then either connections have been deliberately cut or the log has been tampered with. These are the only logical explanations for the data."

"Could it be related to the tachyon field?" Harry Kim asked innocently. "At this level could it be creating interference in our internal systems?"

"It shouldn't be," B'Elanna Torres replied, her voice less firm than usual. "But it makes more sense than sabotage."

"Getting to the bottom of this is our second priority," the captain stated, interrupting the brainstorming she usually encouraged among her staff. "The first thing we have to do is stop this ship from getting any closer to whatever is causing this. Which means bypassing the computer and doing a manual shutoff. I know there are protocols for this . . ."

"I've already tried to access them," Torres interrupted flatly. "They're unavailable."

"Unavailable?" the captain asked, tilting her head slightly as she often did when she found something utterly absurd.

"That's the answer I got. Unavailable. That I

didn't have the proper authorization," the engineer explained.

The captain didn't waste a minute; she requested that the computer access the shutoff protocols.

And she got the same reply. "Those instructions are unavailable without proper authorization," the computer said.

Janeway's eyes burned with fury. "This is Captain Kathryn Janeway, and I am in command of the *Starship Voyager*. I have complete authorization to require any file aboard this vessel."

"Authorization denied," the computer replied.

Janeway met Tuvok's eyes across the table. "Sabotage," the Vulcan said. Then he turned his steady gaze onto the half-Klingon chief engineer. "We need to investigate immediately."

"We need to cut the power immediately," the captain countered him. "That comes first. Once we're not running at warp speed into who-knows-where, we can investigate." She turned her attention to the engineer.

"All right, we'll need to go to manual override," the captain said. "What's the best way to do that?"

Torres's whole body strained with concentration. She stood and leaned on her arms, her elbows stiff and her palms flat on the table. "The only way to do that quickly and effectively is to physically go in and cut the control interfaces at the central box. But that will entirely disable navigation. It'll take several hours to repair once we have this all cleared up."

Janeway nodded. "Can you cut the warp drive without affecting impulse power?"

This time Torres nodded vigorously. "That's easy. The control routings are shunted in completely separate sequences. I'll get right on it."

"Good," the captain said, and rose.

The rest of the staff rose with her, and Torres didn't wait for anyone before she tore out to the turbolift. As the other officers left the ready room, Tuvok lingered behind. The captain knew he wanted to talk to her privately. And she appreciated his discretion almost as much as she valued his intelligence.

As usual, he waited until they were entirely alone before he spoke. "Captain, have you considered that B'Elanna Torres might be the saboteur? She has the expertise and the access. Of any member of this crew, she is the most capable."

Captain Janeway raised her hand as if to wave the suggestion away. "What would she get out of it, Mr. Tuvok?" she asked rhetorically. "She doesn't have any more connection with whatever is in that tachyon field than we do. She has no motive."

Janeway sat back in her chair, her hands steepled in front of her as she considered what her security officer had just told her.

"You really think B'Elanna is doing this to us?" the captain asked, perplexed.

"I have no opinions at this time," the Vulcan answered. "I merely point out that she has the ability and the access. She could have done it.

There are several others who have similar training, though not her particular talent for machinery. And it has happened before."

Yes, there had been earlier sabotage aboard *Voyager*. That had been very difficult for Janeway. As much as the crew had to trust her, she had to trust them as well.

She certainly knew she could trust B'Elanna's competence as an engineer. But it wasn't just competence. It was inspiration. Janeway knew she was fortunate to have found a chief engineer who could combine creativity and passion with warp cores and impulse engines.

Still, B'Elanna was young and half Klingon. She was impulsive in the extreme and often needed to be reined in. Janeway trusted Torres's intentions, but she wasn't quite as sure of the younger woman's judgment in nonmechanical matters.

"I don't know that B'Elanna Torres could, let alone would, practice deception," Janeway said after some consideration.

"As I said, Captain, she is the obvious choice. She has the ability and the access. And if she is not our saboteur, then whoever is doing this has skills that we do not acknowledge and wants to make it look like someone else." Tuvok stopped for a moment to consider. "Therefore, if we behave as if we believe it is Torres, we will either catch her or we will throw whoever is doing this off guard, which will be necessary to catch the perpetrator."

The captain thought about that. "It is logical,"

she began, "but we can't do it. I want you to investigate, but quietly. I don't want anyone to know there is even suspicion of foul play."

"As you like, Captain," Tuvok assented. "But would you explain your reasoning to me?"

"It's very simple, Mr. Tuvok. People who think they're under suspicion are not going to give their very best efforts. And to get out of this we're going to need the best from everyone."

Chakotay was pleased when the captain returned to the bridge. Usually he enjoyed the time he spent in command, reminding him of the days when he commanded his own ship. This time he had not. He had managed some control over his thoughts so that he could function, but the emotional turmoil still raged inside him. He needed to be alone, somewhere where he could have the silence to seek guidance. The bridge was not the place at all.

But he was not left to silence. "Chakotay, would you go down to Engineering and help Ms. Torres with the warp coil connection?" the captain asked. It was not a request, it was an order, and Chakotay knew it. But he was surprised when Tuvok came over to him as he was about to call the turbolift.

"The captain wants you down there to watch what is going on. There is some suspicion of sabotage," the security officer told him. "If you could check as the work is in progress perhaps you will find evidence that something is amiss."

"Wait a minute," Chakotay said, trying to keep

his voice as hushed as the Vulcan's. "Are you saying that you suspect *my* people? You served with them, you know who they are. And none of them has betrayed this ship, and none of them will."

Tuvok looked at him quizzically. "I did not specify who we think may be responsible. At this point we have no evidence. We do not even know that it is sabotage, only that the conditions we have observed could have been created by someone with enough knowledge and access to the engines. It is merely reasonable to investigate."

Chakotay got into the turbolift without further conversation. He would not dignify what he thought was yet another slur on the Maquis officers who had been integrated into *Voyager*'s crew.

When he arrived he found Engineering in a state of controlled frenzy. Teams were stationed at each of the computer control boards, one member underneath and others holding tools and doing diagnostics. Open toolboxes lay gutted on the deck as crew members in gold uniforms rooted through the piles of contraptions that Chakotay could not begin to name. Once in a while one person would hand another some device or change a setting and try again. B'Elanna Torres was nowhere to be seen.

He heard her before he saw her, demanding the smaller laser torch from a teammate he identified as Lieutenant Carey. He was gratified and surprised that she would choose her old rival as her workmate.

"There aren't any smaller sizes," Carey said.

"What do you want me to do, go to sickbay and get a laser scalpel?"

B'Elanna emerged from under a workstation, a grim smile on her face. "Good idea," she said. "Maybe a bunch of them so everyone can have one. These interfaces are tiny, and I don't want to have to cut any more than we need to." She turned her attention to the entire Engineering staff. "Everybody, remember, everything we cut today we're going to have to rebuild. So be selective. Work fast and work accurate, but don't overdo it. We're going to have to stretch supplies and replicator power enough as it is to get this system back on-line."

"Did you really mean that about the scalpels?" Carey asked.

B'Elanna seemed confused. "Of course. It was a brilliant idea."

Lt. Carey shook his head. "I'd hate to face down the doc for those," he said.

"I'll go," Chakotay volunteered.

That was when Torres, Carey, and the rest of Engineering realized that the exec was on deck.

"But, Commander, isn't that a waste of your time?" Torres asked.

Chakotay smiled. "Mr. Carey is an engineer and belongs down here. And I think I can convince The Doctor to give me the supplies. Besides, it will get me out of the stench."

Carey grinned and shrugged. Cutting through interfaces with laser torches really did create an unpleasant aroma, acrid and harsh on nasal membranes.

He still felt very strange, alienated even from B'Elanna, with whom he had served in the Maquis and whom he had mentored through her tempestuous career.

And then the absurdity hit him. There was something very wrong if he felt alienated from B'Elanna, utterly unconnected and unwanted by someone he valued so highly. Someone he knew valued him.

And now he felt vaguely threatened. Paranoid, even, worried about what she might be thinking or planning.

This made no sense. He had been thinking about his feelings, wondering why he was ill at ease. And there was no real problem outside his head. The loneliness wasn't linked to anything in real life at all.

This had nothing to do with him, Chakotay realized. There was something else wrong. Maybe the intuition that made it clear that no matter what the orders, the ship was heading straight into the tachyon field was giving him new information.

Only without the proper quiet and peace of mind he couldn't use it, couldn't follow the threads into the spirit world where he could see it all very distinctly.

Someone jostled him and muttered a perfunctory apology, racing back to another work crew. He tried to step out of the way, only to find himself walking over a set of implements of various size and color whose function he could not identify.

"Commander, could you pass me the two millimeter containment jib?" a young ensign asked.

Chakotay moved aside so that she could choose the tool herself. He was definitely in the way here.

If he had some possible insight into the problem, something that might get them out of trouble, it was his duty to follow it as seriously as possible. When he was captain, he hadn't cared where the information had come from, so long as it was useful. And he certainly would have insisted that one of his senior officers with such a feeling follow it up and get whatever could be found.

Deciding that he would talk to the captain as soon as he could made him feel better. The loneliness was still there, debilitating if acknowledged. But he didn't pay attention. Get to sickbay. Get the scalpels. That was more useful than anything else he could do on the crowded Engineering deck.

The thoughts occupied him in the turbolift until he arrived at sickbay, where he was greeted by The Doctor and Kes, both preparing for the worst. First aid supplies, normally stowed in cabinets, were laid out ready on tables. Medical tricorders and other equipment that was strangely reminiscent of the tools strewn across the flooring in Engineering was arranged next to bandages and a rank of prefilled hyposprays.

"Yes, what's the matter, Commander?" The

Doctor asked, visually examining the exec for any overt signs of trauma.

"Engineering needs several laser scalpels," he said.

"I don't have any to spare," The Doctor replied. "The charges are low, and we've been put on alert. Medical supplies are a top priority."

Chakotay didn't want to argue. This was absurd. "You've got to be able to spare a couple," he said. "I know that last month Ensign Ortega used one for an art project."

"And didn't return it. Why don't you go hunt down Ensign Ortega? We have work to do, if you don't mind."

Chakotay was about to turn and leave, feeling as if the effort to understand what had been going on had been futile. He was engulfed again, and worse. The Doctor turned his back and went to the office.

Chakotay went back to the door when Kes came up to him and touched his arm lightly. "You have to forgive him," she said softly. "The strain is getting to everyone. Come, I'll give you a few of the larger scalpels. We don't have many Ordanu or Karesi in this quadrant to use them on."

For the first time since they had entered the tachyon field, Chakotay smiled. "I've never even seen an Oradanu or Karesi, not the whole time I was in Starfleet. I think they don't get out much."

Kes handed over three wrapped packages. "If this won't do, come back and talk to me. I'm sure I can find things that aren't vital to sickbay."

Chakotay thanked Kes warmly. He had had little interaction with the Delta Quadrant native. Their duties didn't intersect and his health was excellent. He hadn't considered her at all really a part of the ship's crew, but was pleased to find himself impressed.

"Okay, people, let's pull the plug," B'Elanna Torres said. And every board at every control station in Engineering went dark. All the colors disappeared and only the plain white worklights lit their forms.

"Well, if the computer's gone crazy, it can't do anything else to us now," Lt. Carey observed.

"Computers don't go crazy," Torres said. "That's just in stories."

They were talking loud enough that most of Engineering could hear them. Without the constant background noise of engines, the place seemed unnaturally quiet, haunted, maybe even dead.

But it was dead, B'Elanna thought. She felt its death as a visceral thing. She was connected to those drives, they lived inside of her, breathed with her.

And now they were silent.

CHAPTER
6

"THE COMPUTER IS CRAZY," CHAKOTAY TOLD THE captain.

They were in her ready room, a comfortable space decorated with antique instruments and artifacts, mementos of various scientific expeditions. Janeway was one of the few command officers who had started out in science. She had never lost the taste for it, and her interests were reflected all around her.

Tuvok, a silent presence behind the captain, raised an eyebrow. "Indeed?" he asked.

"It's the tachyon field. It has somehow affected either basic function or communications through the consoles, but essentially what it means is that the computer is not responding in the normal pattern."

Captain Janeway smiled at that. "Well, we knew it wasn't a normal pattern, but I hadn't considered that the tachyon field might be disturbing our internal communications."

"What about neural gel-packs in our computer? Maybe that's where the sabotage is. Someone may have figured out how to do a program override and it's broadcasting," Chakotay insisted. "There was nothing I could see that would lead to the idea that there was real sabotage involved. These gel-packs are the most likely candidate."

"I concur," the captain said softly, after a brief pause. She looked up sharply at her first officer. "We haven't been able to get at the instructions that were in that pack. We don't know what it could have contained."

"They could not know how to program, or reprogram, on that level," Tuvok stated. "It takes years to train a programmer. There is no way anyone here could know our languages."

"But logic is the same," the captain said softly. "And the logical connections would transfer easily."

Then she turned and studied Chakotay. She noticed the dark circles under his eyes and the tension in his mouth. "Commander, how long have you been on this shift?" she asked suddenly.

"Twenty hours, Captain," the exec replied calmly.

"Get some rest, Commander" Janeway said. "Now. And that's an order."

It seemed for a moment as if Chakotay might protest. Then he left the ready room, presumably for his own quarters.

"I am still not convinced, Captain," Tuvok said. "Computers do not 'lose their minds,' and there is no way some race unknown to us could learn to program that quickly. And Commander Chakotay has always been very protective of the former Maquis."

"So you still think that it is sabotage," Janeway said.

"I still think it is the most logical alternative," Tuvok confirmed. "I cannot think of another that has as high a probability."

Janeway smiled wearily. "I have relied on you for a long time," she said softly. "And I value your judgment. We will continue to pursue this line of questioning discreetly. But we will also have to start looking for some other possible explanations, because this strikes me as a very illogical sabotage. Why would any of our people want us any closer to this tachyon field? We don't even know what's there, and whatever it is has Neelix terrified."

"Captain, many things create a strong reaction in Neelix. If he is a prime example of Talaxians, they are a highly emotional people," the Vulcan observed dryly.

This time, real humor touched Janeway's smile. "That may be true, Tuvok, but he knows the region better than the rest of us. And I have no reason to doubt that whatever is inside that field could well be more dangerous to us than we realize."

"Agreed, Captain," Tuvok said.

Janeway led the way out of the ready room and back to the bridge of *Voyager*. The bridge crew glanced up at her and returned their attention to their stations, their faces shadowed with the colored lights of their control panels.

She noted the tense, worried expressions of her staff. They were scared, but they were maintaining discipline.

The symptoms of distress under strict restraint filled her with pride. This was an exceptional crew. Though lost and despairing of home, they still worked with precision and attention to every detail.

"Captain, the readings still indicate that we are traveling at warp," Tom Paris interrupted her musing. "That shouldn't be possible, should it?"

"Is that a passive reading or computer-generated output?" the captain asked quickly.

"Computer generated, Captain," Paris replied.

Janeway could almost hear the relief from Tuvok. "No, Mr. Paris," she said. "The computer still thinks that it's in charge of things, and so it is driving this ship at warp. But with the connections cut, it should effectively be out of the loop. Mr. Tuvok, will you confirm with Engineering that we are traveling at only impulse power?"

Before the Vulcan could say anything, B'Elanna Torres stepped out of the turbolift and onto the bridge. Energy crackled around her as she strode briskly to report.

"Captain," she said. "We cut every connection and the warp core should be off-line. But we're still generating power, and the ship is still headed toward the middle of that field. And we're slower than we were before, but we're not down to a stop yet."

"Why not?" Janeway asked, perturbed.

"I don't know why not," the engineer said furiously. "According to everything I know about power control, that warp core should be cold." She practically spat out the last word, as if the fact that there was still some drive power left was a personal insult.

"Do you think there could be some kind of tractor beam pulling us in?" Harry Kim asked ingenuously. "Or maybe there's something very dense in there so we're feeling the gravitation as well."

"For it to be dense enough to be affecting us at this level, it would have to be a black hole," Torres shot back. "And we aren't getting any readings that indicate any serious mass in this region at all. Only those old dead ships out there."

"Maybe they're not so dead," Paris interjected.

And suddenly the bridge was enveloped in dark. Not a single control panel was lit, and the giant forward screen was dead black. Even the service lights had died.

"Sit tight, people," Janeway said. She couldn't

see anyone, but at least there were no footsteps sounding. Before she could say anything more, the screen lit up like a nova before them. And when she had recovered her sight through the red and yellow flash dots that floated in her retinas, Janeway saw a clear communication on the screen.

She sat up straighter. "I am Captain Kathryn Janeway of the Federation ship *Voyager*. We come in peace and mean you no harm."

The beings did not seem to respond to this greeting. They were so close to human that it was hard to see the immediate differences. And they were not only fully humanoid, but all spectacularly beautiful. Perfect bodies with sculpted muscles under faces so refined that the only image Janeway could think of was angels.

They all had different coloring; there was one with pale blue hair and matching eyes and skin the color of new snow, one with honey skin and golden hair, another with skin the shade of the midnight sky and hair sparkling silver white like the stars twinkling in the distance. Their semitranslucent garments draped fluidly, and with hair and skin all the colors of an artist's palette, it was sometimes hard to discern what was flesh and what was clothing.

"We of the ship *Lys* are in desperate need of assistance," said the woman with the indigo skin. Her voice was as fluid and mellifluous as her robe. "You are no doubt aware of the tachyon field that surrounds us. It makes communication and readings very difficult. Please, we beg you, come rescue us. Our drive is destroyed and we are in danger. Please help us. Please come."

It's a real signal, all right, Captain," Harry Kim said.

"Kind of odd how it's coming through the tachyon field when nothing else could," Tom Paris added. "And we're still heading for them whether we want to or not. Only, Captain, we're not at warp speed any more. In fact, we're on low impulse."

"Oh," B'Elanna Torres's voice was unmistakable in the dark. "The warp core's cool-down phase is on long duration. We did that to conserve power."

"But it's still dark," Tom Paris pointed out as the lights came back on.

"I'd guess that the message was punched way up to get through the interference and overloaded the screen circuits," Ensign Kim conjectured.

"Another thing we'll have to fix," Torres responded as if she were already on the second page of her list of repairs.

"How much longer until we're in scanner range?" Janeway asked.

"An hour, four minutes," Paris responded quickly. "At normal scan. But with all this interference, I don't know that we'll be able to get decent readings."

"Lieutenant Torres, could you use that hour to configure the scanners to filter the tachyon field?" Janeway suggested.

"I can try it, Captain," the engineer replied. "I'm not sure it'll work, though. Tachyons are so high energy and invasive that they're harder to filter than most other interference."

"What if we do a quantum reset?" Kim asked suddenly, obviously interested in the project. "I read a paper about that right before we left. It's a kind of new use of an old technology, but it sounded really promising."

"Mr. Kim, accompany Lieutenant Torres back to Engineering and give her whatever assistance you can," the captain ordered. "I want to scan these ships as soon as possible for life-forms and find out just how dangerous the conditions are for these people. If there really are any people," she added under her breath.

Just stepping onto the holodeck made Kes sick to her stomach. It was much too real. She could taste the grit in the arid air, she could smell the stench of the other captives and the Kazon who guarded them. She could barely remember that she had had plenty of water earlier in the day and a shower besides and enough to eat.

This was a hideous mistake. She didn't want to think that The Doctor had prescribed the wrong treatment, but she wanted to leave the holodeck right now. There was no point in going through with this. It would only make everything worse.

"Hey, you, back to work," one of the Kazon

guards grunted as he prodded her with his blast rifle.

"Oh, that one," the guard's superior said, laughing. "Let her come here if she's too lazy to dig. These Ocampa are fragile anyway. They don't last very long. But she's a looker."

The guard growled at his superior, and the superior shot the guard. Not killed, but winged badly enough to make him obey orders.

The the superior came over to Kes as she tried to fade back into the dark mine entrance. If she could get into the dark . . . she knew her way around the tunnels and wasn't disoriented by being underground. In fact, she felt contempt for the pirate chasing her. He'd never be able to follow if she got out of the light, and if he did get to her, she'd kill him. She swore it, she'd kill him somehow.

She slipped into the tunnels, forgotten mazes that riddled the surface rock of her home planet. She was silent, her bare feet soft on the smooth rock and dust below her. The guard clomped behind in thick boots, calling for her.

As if she'd answer, she thought. Disdain for his stupidity filled her along with the anger. She had to be careful, she knew. Underestimating the enemy would only lead to mistakes. She couldn't afford a mistake.

She crouched low. There was almost no light at all, but she could hear so clearly that she knew when the guard hit her corridor. She stayed down, silent, her breathing very slow and careful. There could be nothing, nothing at all to give her away.

She could feel the heat of him as he approached, smell his skin. The Kazon bathed no more frequently than their prisoners here, and his odor was as easy to follow as his heavy, labored breathing.

She waited while he passed her. That was the hardest part. She could smell his boots as he came by. She was afraid, terribly afraid. But the fear seemed farther away than the rage. That filled her, gave her courage.

He went past, scuffling a little in the abandoned shaft. Just a little more, to where the rock ledge stuck out . . .

Kes pounced low, slamming his knees with her shoulder. He went down flailing, shrieking. She grabbed his sidearm, turned it upside down, and used the heavy grip on the back of his head. He fell silent.

Quickly she checked his pulse. He was still alive. Kes was almost disappointed. Fury filled her, and she touched the trigger mechanism of the weapon, wondering if she should just shoot. Her outrage demanded justification.

Caution prevailed. If she killed him they would find out. She slipped away. He would never report it. He would be too ashamed. And she still had the weapon, fully charged. Quickly she concealed it under her tunic. Only then did she realize that she was shaking with pure rage.

Kes realized that she'd forgotten the rage. That she had suppressed it, that she hadn't felt lonely at all. No, she had felt angry. Angry, and very afraid, but ready to defend herself no matter what she needed to do.

This was the holodeck on *Voyager,* she told herself. Everything she had experienced was part of the past. It lived in memory, even her anger was only a memory. There were no Kazon here. As she tried to calm herself in cool darkness, she heard footsteps.

"Don't try it," she said, amazed at the menace her voice carried.

"It's me," The Doctor answered. "It seems that you have experienced a therapeutic catharsis before I could even begin to take notes." He sounded disappointed.

"Program off, keep medical hologram running," The Doctor ordered.

"And some furniture, a sofa and some chairs," Kes suggested.

The holosuite complied. "Do you want me to lie down?" Kes asked.

"No, I don't believe that's necessary," The Doctor replied. They both sat down before he continued. "You reacted very strongly in there. You showed a great deal more defiance and courage than anyone could have expected."

"I'm surprised at it myself," Kes agreed. "The odd thing is, in my dream I was terribly, horribly lonely. All I wanted was someone to talk to. And here, today, all I wanted was to kill him." She shuddered delicately at the thought and perched uneasily on the edge of a light green chair.

The Doctor sat down facing her from the sofa. He clasped his hands on his lap and waited for her to continue. Kes took a deep breath and began again.

"The real question is, I don't recall feeling lonely at all," she said slowly. "In the real memories I was angry and afraid and determined. So why did I dream about feeling lonely? Why was that so important?"

The Doctor looked at her quizzically. "There could be several explanations for that. It could be that you're feeling isolated here on *Voyager,* and you can't accept that, so you're trying to assign the feelings to another part of your life."

Kes blinked in surprise. "But I'm not isolated at all here," she said. "I have more friends than I've ever had in my life. You're a wonderful friend and a teacher. And I'm with Neelix. No, that doesn't fit."

"Odd," The Doctor countered. "Among the more empathic races, this kind of reaction is often considered to be generated outside the subject. But we don't know for sure if the Ocampa are empathic." Kes settled into her chair and paused to consider The Doctor's remarks. There were traditional Ocampa stories that sounded like the kind of empathic experiences of Betazoids. And it was well known that Betazoids could mistake others' projected emotions for their own, if they were not properly trained.

"According to Jarzeman Anla, the classical Betazoid authority on empathic behavior, if you try to think of the feelings as outside of yourself, as something you are receiving rather than generating, you will have some distance from them. The feelings will not go away, but they won't affect you so strongly." The Doctor stood up abruptly. He seemed ready to end the session. But Kes wasn't. Not yet.

"What if they are my feelings?" she asked quickly.

"Then the exercise shouldn't affect you at all," The Doctor reassured her rather too briskly. "Now, if you'll excuse me," he continued, making a face. "I undoubtedly have some ski injuries awaiting me in sickbay." Kes barely acknowledged The Doctor as he exited the holodeck. She was too busy considering his suggestion. He was right, thinking could not hurt her. And even if it could, she had stood up to bigger, to stronger adversaries. Surely nothing in her own head could mean her as much harm as the Kazon!

That clear to her, she began. She had never done anything remotely like this before, but it seemed as easy and natural as walking or breathing. The strange feelings that were without a rational source were somehow separate from the rest of her thinking. She imagined a box around them, an Ocampa party box covered in pink cloth and decorated with fresh white flowers.

She had been given such a box once, by her parents on the occasion of her maturity. It had contained her great-grandmother's necklace, her naming bracelet, and a reader-player with all the most obscure traditional songs, each performed and annotated. She wondered where the box and its contents were now. She had had them with her in a bundle when she had taken the tunnels to the surface.

The bundle had disappeared. Maybe it had been recovered by another of the traditional rebels. Or maybe the Kazon had it, which would mean that the jewelry was sold or adorned some ragged pirate, and that the reader-player was trash. That made her sad in a way that had nothing to do with the strange emotions at all.

In fact, she could clearly feel the difference between this thought, which came from her own authentic life, and the feelings now wrapped in the box that had nothing at all to do with her.

She hesitated telling The Doctor. She wasn't sure that she wanted to know she was an empath like a Betazoid. That would make her a thing again, the way she had been in the mines. And she was through with that forever.

Besides, if the feelings were not hers, she would have to discover whose they were. She was suddenly worried that they were Neelix's. That made sense. They were deeply bonded, and he was central to her life. He had rescued her, been brave for her sake.

If this was his trouble she was experiencing, she didn't want to reveal it. Not to anyone. Not ever.

CHAPTER
7

"WE'RE IN SCANNER RANGE," PARIS ANNOUNCED.

"Then take a look, and let's see if there really are any life-forms in that—mess," Janeway said.

There really was no other word for it. *Ship,* at least to a Starfleet officer, meant something space-worthy. Whatever was out there certainly was not. Even from this distance and with all the interference, and the screen jury-rigged besides, it was obvious that this was not something any sensible Federation teenager would buy cut-rate from a Ferengi.

What was discernible of the metal was dark and matte. It wasn't black or really blue either, but some indecipherable shade in between. A few markings in bright orange were scattered over the main cylindrical segment, but were so worn and pitted that the original shapes of the letters or images were not clear.

At least in design it was recognizable. The main segment was a simple cylinder. The other pieces were all curved and curled, and it was impossible to tell what their original alignment on the alien ship had been.

"It" was too specific, actually. There were several pieces, or things, all different designs as if they had been trashed together in the sector junk heap well after any usefulness had been sucked out of them. At least one was ripped open to cold space and the tachyon bombardment that seemed to be coming from the central object in the collection. This one was smaller than many of the ships around it, more compact, and looked as if it had taken less damage.

"Looks like the aftermath of a battle," Tom Paris said to no one.

He was right, it did look like the debris left by a skirmish, now ancient and lost to history. Perhaps these warriors had been dead when Earth itself was still covered by primal seas. Prehistoric space battles in skies that the Federation had never seen, for planets that might now be as dead and cold as the hulks outside.

But they were far distant from any planetary base. They were far enough from any star system that supplies were a problem. If this was a moment of truth from the storybooks, it had drifted well away from its origin.

"Mr. Neelix, come up to the bridge," Janeway

said into her comm badge. "There's something you might be able to identify."

"The scans aren't reading clearly," Paris said. "It looks like a negative, then there's tachyon interference, and it spikes into the positive range. Always in the same place, as if whatever life is there is concentrated in one area."

He hesitated and looked up from his console, turned and faced the captain. "I don't trust it, Captain," he said. "The negatives are too clear too close to that area. The particle bombardment could be giving us false readings."

The captain used her commbadge again, this time to Engineering. "Can you filter out more of the interference?" she asked. "There's still too much coming through for us to get a clear reading."

"We're doing our best, Captain," Torres replied. "The field is fluctuating pretty violently here. Once I match it, it seems to jump again."

"Do what you can," the captain said, knowing full well that Torres and Kim were doing more than anyone else could imagine. Still, she was frustrated and intrigued at the same time. The curiosity that had made her a good science officer was full of questions and speculations about what could be going on.

The screen sputtered again, and again cleared to the interior of a ship filled with the people who were colored like Christmas angels. In fact, this time she saw a green-haired, silver-skinned one and one with skin as red as her uniform with glossy black hair.

Somehow Janeway had the impression she had seen something like them before somewhere, she just couldn't place it. And they were both so beautiful and so bizarre that it seemed very odd to her that she couldn't recall where she'd seen anything like them before.

Unless it was in some kind of painting, perhaps.

The indigo-skinned one came forward again. "Please hurry," the being said, pleading. "We need your help. Please. We can direct you in. We can take you over if you like."

"Won't the tachyon bombardment and fluctuations interfere with your transport device?" Janeway demanded.

"We are adapted to this phenomenon," the indigo angel said softly. "But of course, if you wish to use your own equipment, we are more than pleased that you do so. We want you to trust us. We need your help."

Something about the way the angel made the statement made Captain Janeway's skin crawl. She didn't know whether it was the neediness in the plea itself or the way in which it was delivered, but she was certain this was no routine rescue.

"We will send over a shuttlecraft as soon as we are within a reasonable range," she said. "Stand by." And she cut the connection.

"What's with a shuttlecraft range, Captain?" Tom Paris asked, confused.

Janeway just smiled. "I think we have a thing or two to learn about our would-be refugees before we go picking them up," she said.

"That's a Tsranan ship, Captain," Neelix said. No one had noticed his arrival. Now it simply was natural that he was there. "Looks like one of their freighters, though I can't say they look like much."

Janeway was slightly startled by his voice. She hadn't heard him come in, hadn't been aware of his presence. She asked if he had seen the message and could identify the race of the people asking for aid.

"I haven't seen anyone like them," Neelix said quickly. "I haven't even heard of anyone like them. A race where no two people have the same color, that's absurd."

"Or cosmetic," Tuvok observed.

"And why would anyone go to all the trouble of that much cosmetic variation when they're in danger?" Janeway asked, more for herself than to elicit a reply.

"Ritual, perhaps," Tuvok said. "Or they mark rank and position by their coloration. Or maybe it's a deeper part of identity. This is known among at least three groups we have contacted, two in the Alpha Quadrant and one in the Gamma Quadrant."

"Or maybe it's something much simpler and closer to home," Janeway mused, turning the idea over in her head and on her tongue at the same time. Then her voice shifted to a stronger one, that of command. "Computer, replay that last transmission without audio. Slow down picture and magnify the faces."

They came on the screen again, each of them perfect, frozen.

"Computer, play this with an image of the earlier transmission."

There was the one with the pale blue hair again, almost overlaid over the red-skinned individual in the last broadcast.

"They could be twins," Paris said. "They're almost identical."

"Not almost, Mr. Paris," the captain corrected him gently. "The faces are the same. Look. Computer, go to black-and-white screen."

And there it was. Without the color, all the angels had one single face.

"There's no indication of any life-forms," Paris said. "We're getting a clear reading now, and there isn't anyone to be rescued." He turned around and looked at the captain. "It's a trap."

Kathryn Janeway smiled. "That much is obvious," she said quietly. "The real question is why whatever set this up is trying to lure people in."

"This must be whatever killed the Rhiellians," Neelix said softly. "He said something about there being people there, beautiful people who were calling to them. Only what a Rhiellian would like is not anything you or I might like, Captain. Rhiellians are six-legged and have an exoskeleton. I wouldn't think they'd be impressed with these images."

"So whatever is there tailors the display to the race it finds," the captain said. "Which means they aren't even looking for a particular kind of sentient being, a single species or even a class. They're looking for whoever's out here."

"Well, this isn't exactly the shopping district of Rigel," Tom Paris said. "You'd have to take what you could get out in the middle of nowhere."

The captain stood and smiled without humor. "It might not always have been the middle of nowhere," she said grimly. "But that doesn't matter now. We just have to get out of here."

She touched her commbadge quickly. "Mr. Kim, meet us in shuttlecraft bay two." Then she turned her attention back to the staff on the bridge. "Mr. Paris, you're with me. We're going to get out of here now."

In the shuttlecraft, Tom Paris took the pilot's seat. Though both the captain and Harry were more than qualified to fly the shuttlecraft, Paris was the best pilot on the ship. The captain expected him to be able to do things that no one else could pull off.

Like fly through this tachyon field that would distort instrument readings and get them to the empty shell that was broadcasting the images. Not an easy task, but one he relished. When he was flying, especially doing something that taxed his skill and his nerve, he was most truly alive. And like many true pilots, he enjoyed flying shuttlecraft as much as he liked being at the controls of *Voyager* herself.

"*Voyager*, do we have any further readings on this broadcast, or on the shell?" Janeway asked as the shuttle peeled away from *Voyager* and darted forward on its own course into the heart of the storm.

"No, Captain, only that the readings we are getting are contradictory and we cannot get a lock on anything substantial," Tuvok said.

Janeway knew that he didn't approve. He was far too disciplined to tell her so, but she knew what he thought. *A captain's place is on the bridge. Always go in fully prepared.*

But she was fully prepared, or as prepared as she could be. And as for being on the bridge, well, that was a captain's place. It was also the captain's place to lead, to go where others might fear, to make first contact, to make decisions.

She would not ask anything of her crew that she would not do first herself. That was something Kathryn Janeway had lived by as long as she had been in Starfleet. She was not about to stop now.

Instead, she watched Tom Paris at the controls. Now he was flying on visual information as much as using his instruments, obviously correcting for the inaccuracies introduced by the tachyon field.

From the copilot's seat she had a good view of the window as well as the control panel. She leaned back in the seat, content to let Paris do his job and to do hers—to watch, observe, understand what was happening around them. And to take care of *Voyager*. Always that came first, her ship.

"You are cleared for exit," the computer voice announced. "Seven seconds until decompression. Six. Five. Four. Three . . ."

The great door of the shuttlebay opened. After the light from the interior, the darkness of space was blinding. Janeway lowered the ambient light level in the shuttle so that they were able to adjust and see what surrounded them.

Large segments of dead spacecraft wheeled aimlessly around them in a ballet choreographed by gravity and velocity and nothing more. Except for the regular shapes and obviously created fragments, this could have been an asteroid belt. But the glimpses of insignia on torn metal, of corrosion on a clean surface, reminded her that this was a graveyard.

The eternal silence of vacuum seemed to have engulfed the shuttle. No one talked as they watched the debris that was the deaths of ships go by.

They were closing now, and Janeway could see the assortment of junk that had become a trash armada. The remains of ships of unimaginable configurations were grouped randomly, so far as she could tell. Some had smashed into each other, others were slowly drifting in their own debris.

Most were white or black or showed mostly the material from which they had been formed. But a few still had bits of bright paint clinging. One was covered with flat orange where abrasion had not sanded it away. Another bore lines of hieroglyphs on every smooth surface.

Then the captain turned her attention to the large hulk near the center. Except for the gash on one side, it appeared to be intact. The outer hull was some matte dark material that glinted with deep blue when light hit it. Almost a match for space itself. Janeway wondered whether this coloring was meant as disguise or as an attempt to honor their environment.

Clearly derelict, there was no reason to even suspect there had been life aboard. The message they had received was strange, a trap set long ago, Janeway suspected. And now the transmissions still went out without anyone who benefitted. And many who had died.

She thought of a spider's web, each of the ships caught by the tachyon field and the distress call. She wondered how the broadcast could be so neatly tailored for each species that visited, and if such a technology could be adapted for her own purposes.

They had run across other hopes before. Just knowing that one people had learned to fold time-space made her think that others must have learned it as well. Not to mention the Caretaker's technology, which was so advanced *Voyager* might as well have been a wooden ship with sails.

No, there was hope out here. And there were things to learn. With no life aboard, whatever she found in these bits of antique flotsam was going to be theirs. She regretted that she hadn't brought

B'Elanna Torres along. The engineer probably would be able to recognize and figure out the workings of some of the more esoteric finds.

But B'Elanna had her hands full with the disconnected drive and whatever additional damage the field had done. Once she had a better idea of what was out here and exactly what they might want to investigate, she could send Torres. Much more efficient that way. Otherwise her chief engineer would want to take apart every moving part in the entire assembly.

"Talk about a bunch of hangar queens," Paris said, interrupting Janeway's thoughts.

"Hangar queens?" Kim asked. Janeway smiled. She hadn't considered that before, but the assumption was obvious.

"A ship that sits in dock so you can cannibalize parts of it to repair everything else," Tom Paris said, smiling. "Kind of like supplies on the hoof. They did it all the time in the Maquis."

"You weren't a Maquis that long," Harry replied.

"Long enough to pick up a few pointers," Paris protested. "Besides, B'Elanna's gonna love this."

"Before we start dividing up the spoils, perhaps we should take a look at what we have," the captain said dryly. "Mr. Paris, take us in nice and easy. I don't want to trigger whatever other traps have been left here."

The pilot smiled and turned the shuttlecraft in an elegant arc around the outer edge of the heap before slowing down and entering the precinct. Here he had to fly as though he were maneuvering through an asteroid belt. The major ships themselves were easy to avoid, but the oversized detritus that had detached from the main array whirled crazily.

Harry Kim sucked in his breath audibly while Paris dodged a couple of particularly nasty looking bits of wreck. The captain was so calm she could have been playing 3-D chess in the *Voyager* lounge.

Paris pulled out suddenly to avoid a wildly spinning bit of flotsam that seemed to be headed straight for them. He hit the acceleration hard across the paths of two major ships to avoid the debris. There was nowhere else to go, not enough time, not enough space to maneuver. He cursed under his breath, his teeth clenched as he swung the ungainly little shuttle across the bows of two enormous hulks.

He yanked the shuttle down and hard port just as the dead weapons of an ancient warrior opened fire.

He had been fast but not quite fast enough. They were jolted from behind as broad beam energy weapons discharged just meters above them.

Paris went into fighter maneuvers, pushing the chunky shuttlecraft to the edge of its limits, stressing the hull with the quick turns and intricate foils designed for fighter craft.

He pulled them to starboard so hard that the captain and Kim were flung against their armrests.

There hadn't been time to tell them to strap down before he began the evasive procedures.

"What was that, Captain?" Kim asked as he got up off the shuttlecraft floor.

"I would suspect an automatic passive trigger," Janeway said, brushing off her trousers and the palms of her hands. "Those were not merchants."

Tom Paris was grinning broadly. "But I pulled us out near the center ship. We should be in the clear now."

"Unless there's something else here to shoot at us," Kim said. "I thought there weren't any life-forms here."

"There aren't," Janeway said. "These were old pieces on automatic. I've heard of traps like this."

"The Cardassians pull this kind of trick all the time," Paris said. "But they have life-forms reading on those ships. Sometimes they bundle people they consider traitors or prisoners together to watch their ship fire passively at their rescuers. Chakotay told me about being in a trap like that once."

Harry Kim looked very anxious.

"Let's get on with our job, gentlemen," the captain's crisp, positive tone wiped away some of the lingering chill of the attack. "Mr. Paris, take us in."

CHAPTER

8

THE BREECH IN THE HULL WAS SO LARGE IT WAS LIKE entering one of the berths at McKinley Station. Tom Paris could do it in his sleep, but after the encounter with the odd attackers, he was grateful for an easier charge. The adrenaline that had rushed through his body during the encounter with the live weapons subsided now, leaving him cold and quivering with a slight metallic taste in his mouth.

The sight before him was awe-inspiring. In the dead vacuum that had preserved the cavity nothing moved. But it was easy to imagine some kind of people here. Where the plating had been torn away, all the decks were open to view.

"They must have been giants," Harry Kim said.

Neither the captain nor Paris answered. They

didn't have to. The cavernlike living and working quarters spoke for themselves under the high illumination from the shuttle.

No furniture was recognizable as such. Each of the spaces had sparkling crystals hanging from the ceilings and more squat, rounded matching pieces projecting from the floor. It looked like a natural formation, like a true cave carved by rivers before time.

"What a sense of beauty," Janeway said softly. "No wonder they appear as beautiful no matter what form they take."

"I don't see anything that looks like a control area or Engineering," Paris said. "It all looks like a cave. B'Elanna's going to have a field day with this one."

"We're too far away to tell," the captain reminded him. "When we get closer, I would bet that several of those projections are very recognizable controls."

"You're on, Captain," both Paris and Kim said together.

The captain smiled. "I think you've both been spending too much time playing pool on the holodeck. What are the stakes?"

Paris smiled evilly. "A cup of real-live Earth-origin coffee," he said.

"You're on," Janeway accepted, grinning.

"Come on, gentlemen," the captain chided them gently. "We don't have the rest of the millennium."

"Well, where should I put her down?" Paris asked, all business again.

"How about there." The captain pointed to a spot that shone brilliantly when the lights of the shuttlecraft hit it. "Looks like there's something important over there."

"It's where I'd put a command center," Paris concurred. "Close to the front and center. Okay, Captain, we're in."

He brought them slowly toward what appeared to be the bright core of a dead command center. In the illumination from the shuttle it was full of high contrast and deep shadow. Nothing made any sense at all except that the reflected radiance at the core didn't really seem to go with the rest of the dark, silent ship. The cave that had become a ship.

"It makes sense," Janeway mused aloud, her scientific curiosity unstoppable even when faced with a threatening enigma. "Troglodytes taking to space. The dark and the isolation wouldn't be difficult for them. It would be a natural extension of their habitat."

Tom Paris ignored the captain's theorizing. As he approached the sheared plating, he found that there was no decent landing site. The entire deck was covered with jagged crystals and large projections upthrust from what appeared to be a fragile crust.

"I'm going to destroy this stuff if I set down on it, Captain," Paris admitted after one good look. "If you think we can risk it, I'll go ahead, but . . ."

"No," Janeway came back quickly. "I don't want to compromise anything that might be part of their technical system. If we can use it, we will. No, let's land three decks down. That's empty, it looks like it might have been a cargo bay or something. Then we'll have to walk."

"In environmental suits," Paris groaned.

It took a few minutes to pull on the suits. Paris hadn't worn one since his training mission at the Academy, and he bet that everyone would have liked to keep it that way.

"How do I get the cooling on this down?" Paris fumed, sweat running down his face.

"Uh, Tom, I'll take care of it," Kim said. "Just let me finish with the captain. They tried to make it easier in this version."

Easier. Right. Tom Paris had heard that before. It wasn't easier, it was a mess. But Harry, more recently at the Academy, was familiar with the new design and got the suits adjusted to a pleasant temperature. Not that being cool enough made it easier to move. It reminded Paris of how his mother had made him wear sweaters under his coat in the winters, and how hard it had been to bend his arms.

"Let's go," the captain said, and led the way out of the shuttle and into the torn alien craft. Her voice came through the helmet speakers and wasn't as clear as the commbadge.

But as soon as they left the shuttlecraft, Paris was too interested to notice his discomfort.

The alien ship was amazing. He had thought it large when he had flown through the gash in her side. Now, standing in what he assumed had to have been a cargo or shuttlebay, he realized that his sense of scale had been wrong. It was not simply large, it was gigantic. These must have been a race of behemoths.

"The alloy is related to steel, but there is a particle in the mixture that the tricorder can't identify," Kim said. Harry had the tricorder while Paris held a phaser in his hand. Not that there could be anything alive here, and the readings had confirmed that, but he felt better with it anyway. The place was so eerie that he wouldn't have been surprised to see a colossal ghost.

The captain didn't linger in the bay. Whatever had been here—cargo, craft, repair supplies, a garden—was gone now, sucked out by the vacuum of space. Or expelled by the internal pressure of an atmosphere the ship no longer had.

Janeway led them to a door that was sealed shut. Harry came over and pointed his tricorder at the complicated looking lock.

"I think it's an airlock, Captain," Kim said, amazement in his voice. "Why would they have an inside airlock?"

"Maybe this was a flight deck," Tom Paris offered. "Then they could open the whole thing to space and pull out quickly in formation."

"Possible," the captain agreed. "But maybe this is an early craft. Most spacegoing people build their first ships in segments with airlocks in between that can be isolated in case of a breech."

Tom Paris raised his phaser to blast open the lock. The captain raised her hand. "Let's not damage this if we don't have to. If it's an early design, it should be fairly straightforward. And there's a good chance it isn't locked. Airlocks are for keeping atmosphere in, not interlopers out."

She stepped toward the lock and ran a gloved hand over a handle easily three times the size of anything Paris had ever seen before. She pushed at it from various angles. Finally, she struck it head on, trying to get the oversize thing to move at all.

"If it's that old, it could be jammed, Captain," Harry started to say as a weak automatic light came on and the door heaved open.

The three of them in their suits fit easily into the middle chamber of the airlock. The outer door shut and it was utterly black inside. "Really *old* design," Kim said, impressed. "I've never even seen this technology before."

Then it was just dark and silent. Time ceased to mean anything, and Paris thought it could have been a minute or ten before the inner door came open onto a corridor where a few lights still made a feeble attempt to brighten the gloom.

But the lights were embedded in the crystals that hung like icicles from the ceiling, and their flickering showed off an array of color that was as beautiful as it was mysterious. Under their feet the surface was smooth and polished between rows of upthrust crystals that lined the walls.

The projections weren't regular at all. The colors varied and the size and shape of each of the projections was unique. Yet, overall they gave the impression of perfected nature. Like his mother's cottage garden, Paris thought. Everything looked like it had been left to happy natural chance, but in fact it was carefully planned. He was impressed.

"Are you getting all this, Mr. Kim?" the captain asked.

Harry replied in the affirmative, turning constantly to capture yet another projection or get some recording of the effect of the whole.

"Do you think we can take the suits off now, Captain?" Paris asked. Now that there was atmosphere, the thing was definitely miserable.

"It's still a hundred below zero in here," Kim answered. "It's amazing that anything at all works here. Unless they were using superconductors."

The corridor took a sharp turn that had been obscured by the projections. When they rounded the corner, they found themselves in front of an interior door. There was no lock here.

"Open sesame," Paris muttered.

The door opened.

"Wait a minute, that isn't supposed to happen," the pilot protested.

"Maybe the suit communicator triggered it," the captain said.

And they were surrounded by the angels again.

The one with the indigo skin and the silver white hair, the Christmas pair and the pale blue one and the one that was shot with gold, they were all there, smiling, welcoming.

And they were tall, but not at all of a size to have built this ship. In fact, they were all about the same size, Paris thought. Taller than he was, but not so much so that they were abnormal for a human. They were still a hair under two meters, Paris was certain of it.

"Thank you for coming to our aid," the indigo-skinned one said. "We have been waiting so very long, and no one comes. We are safe in here from the thing that waits. Here we can be at home. You must come here and stay, all of you."

"What thing that waits?" the captain asked. Though her voice sounded neutral, Tom Paris caught the note of disbelief in her tone. The captain was having none of them, he thought. And neither was he.

"Captain, nothing is registering on the tricorder. Not on any life reading at all. I've adjusted it for other compositions, including metallic, and the only thing I'm getting is energy concentration and coherent light."

"Gentlemen, we've reached the holodeck," the captain announced. "I thought it would have to be something like this. Created especially for us."

"That's more sophisticated than that simple airlock would indicate," Harry Kim said.

"And they're not big enough for this ship," Paris added. "They aren't to scale around here."

"It is beautiful here, and everything is provided. And it is safe. You can stay here and have everything, and that which waits will be satisfied. It will not harm you. It has no wish to harm if we do not interfere with its needs." The indigo-skinned one made the little speech.

"Well, we would like to see the rest of the ship," Janeway said, and went back for the door again.

Only there was no door. It had disappeared, along with all the walls and the strange projections. In its place was a small pond with goldfish flickering under the surface and violet lilies blooming on their pads. One of the angels, this one colored turquoise and red, sprinkled what appeared to be crumbs over the water. They were in the middle of a garden with a fountain on the far side and carved white benches around a small table. Pink creeper roses covered a large sycamore tree that dripped down over a picnic blanket where several of the angels were setting out food no one on *Voyager* had seen in months.

A single crystal bowl held fresh pineapple and mandarin oranges and pears. An entire turkey on a silver platter took pride of place, but it was surrounded by bread and several decanters of wine and plates full of spinich pies and rice and Tuscan white beans in rosemary.

"Come, take off those suits. It is pleasant here,"

the indigo one said. "You can enjoy a repast, and then we can make arrangements."

"Mr. Paris," Captain Janeway's voice cut like ice through the soporific blandishments of the aliens. "Your phaser. Now."

He didn't need to be told twice. He turned away from the images of the beings and opened fire at full power.

Nothing happened. The phaser had been fully charged before he left *Voyager*. He had checked. He knew he wanted to be armed on this mission, and he wouldn't leave a thing like that to chance. But it should be working.

Maybe it was too cold, maybe the internal synapses of the phaser had frozen.

That was ridiculous. Phasers didn't freeze. Phasers that worked two hours ago still worked.

So he shot again, a protracted blast that ran the power gauge down two notches.

"According to the tricorder, there's a big smoking hole where Tom just shot," Harry said incredulously.

"Well, let's just walk out and see what happens," Janeway said. She turned away from the images of the people who weren't there at all, walked straight into the sycamore, and disappeared from sight behind the creeper roses.

"You are making a great mistake," the indigo angel said after her. "But if you return, we will try to help you. No one survives here without help. No one can outfight it. We can only accept what we can have here and enjoy it. You will return. We shall be glad to see you."

Paris and Kim followed the captain into the tree. When they reached it, they found they could walk through it easily. Turning around, they saw shreds of the garden through a haze, as if there were a curtain of mist forming where the wall had been.

"It seems to be repairing itself, Captain," Kim said, looking at the tricorder. "It's completely inorganic, but there's an energy field forming and—seems to be creating a matrix for matter."

"Maybe there's something in that we could use," Janeway said briskly. She looked around briefly. "This isn't the way we came in." Then she struck out down another hallway through the projecting crystal light.

CHAPTER
9

ENGINEERING WAS DARK AND DISEMBOWELED, CHAK-otay thought as he motioned to B'Elanna Torres to follow him to a more private corner. For some reason the dark made it seem hushed as well, though several work crews were engaged in repair operations. It seemed they were talking only in hushed whispers, as if with the warp core that was the center of their lives dead and dark, they were at a funeral. The harsh emergency lights and hand lanterns created an eerie chiaroscuro effect that reinforced the whole atmosphere of untimely death.

Chakotay could tell that B'Elanna Torres was upset. Not simply angry but confused on top of it. She hated being confused. He had rarely seen her having trouble understanding the nature of a problem.

This was not one of those times. She didn't look at him as she spoke, she studied her readout instead as if that would finally provide the revelation.

"I've run a level four diagnostic," she said before he could begin. "I've checked every single one of those connections we cut. This does not make sense. The computer is functioning properly, the connections were all working on the correct interface. According to all the tests, there's nothing wrong." She spat out the last few words as if they tasted bad.

"But there's still a problem," Chakotay said, trying to get her to go over all the details. Not that he would find a solution that she couldn't see. His talents were limited when it came to engineering. But if B'Elanna heard it one more time, she might find some insight.

And then she could fix whatever was wrong and they could leave.

That was Chakotay's goal, to have the ship running on full power and under their guidance by the time the captain returned from the away mission. He had thought it was a fairly straightforward task. Now he wasn't so sure.

"There's a big problem," Torres said, and sighed heavily. "The computer doesn't acknowledge that there was any error in navigation coming to this place." She sighed and tapped her fingers on the console. "You know, I used to trust computers. They aren't like people, they don't do things for stupid reasons, like they like the way you wear your hair or the color of the sky today is orange. But this computer isn't behaving like that. It feels almost as if I'm dealing with an irrational biological being who has all kinds of selfish reasons for making trouble."

"And that's the best I can figure out so far. Mechanically, the thing is working just fine. But this is deeper than mechanics. I have this sense that I'm being lied to."

Chakotay nodded. He understood the feeling very well, even if attributing it to a computer was not going to get them anywhere. "Let's start with something easier," he said. "How about reconnecting all the station interfaces in Engineering? Do we have enough supplies for that? I don't want to start the work until we've tracked down the bug in the program that's causing the problem, but we have to be ready. The captain is going to want us out of here immediately."

Torres nodded briskly and looked relieved. This, at least, was a problem Chakotay knew she could handle.

"We've got the supplies, but the number three phase alignment threads are low on power, and this job is going to take a lot of them. I thought about bleeding power off the residual on the power-down, but that's at too high a level. It'll melt the threads."

She shook her head. "I have this idea that we could tap into that jury-rig contraption that Neelix calls his oven, but I don't want to deal with the hassles."

"Or the dinners." Chakotay's eyes crinkled up as he shared a warm laugh with B'Elanna.

"Neelix shouldn't be a problem," the first officer reassured the engineer. "He knows we're short on energy, and that oven is very inefficient."

"I can offer to calibrate it for him, as well as improve the efficiency," Torres said, smiling. "He won't know what someone's doing in there with the tools. And it will work better after we're done."

"Problem solved," Chakotay agreed. But then his smile faded. "That still doesn't solve the bigger problem of what went wrong with the computer, and we have to have an answer to it. If the regular diagnostic doesn't show the problem, can we access the actual code? Maybe we could isolate whatever was in that burst from the tachyon field. Everything was working just fine until then."

Torres pursed her lips in thought. "I can try it. But I need the best programmer on this ship. And for my money, that's Harry Kim."

"Who's on the away team," Chakotay finished for her. The second in command considered the problem. "There's Ensign Mandel. She may be even better than Harry when it comes to this level of code. I'll send her down."

"Oh? What department is she in?" Torres asked. The engineer couldn't keep the skepticism out of her voice. After all, a truly fine programmer would have to be on the engineering team, and she knew the qualifications of every person in her department.

"Stellar Cartography," Chakotay replied.

Torres nearly snorted. "Figures," she said. "They always nab the top programmers first. Why didn't I think of it?"

Chakotay smiled warmly. B'Elanna Torres was the best engineer he had ever worked with, but she was still young, and her people skills could use some improvement.

Though she had come a long way from when she had decked Carey, he thought. She hadn't done anything even close for months. "You won't have any trouble with Mandel. Your management skills are improving so much that by the time we get home, you'll be ready for the Diplomatic Service," Chakotay said approvingly.

The first officer got up and left B'Elanna to her station. He felt warmed and reassured, even though he hadn't felt any need for reassurance. Which was curious. Usually he was happiest solving the problems of the day, saddest when he thought about home and all they missed.

Maybe it was solving B'Elanna's problem of finding a programmer that made him happy, he thought. In fact, there was no reason why he couldn't send Mandel down immediately. He used his comm badge to order the ensign to report to Engineering.

But solving the problem in Engineering was only the first item to resolve on this watch. He wanted a lot more done by the time the captain returned home.

Ensign Daphne Mandel was not pleased to report to Engineering. She had other work to do, important work. The kind of thing she had dreamed of doing but had never believed could really happen. A whole new, unexplored quadrant for her to map.

Oh, if she was lucky, she had once thought, she might eventually get assigned to Deep Space Nine as one of the cartographers working on the Gamma Quadrant. Even with maps from the people there, there was a lot of work to do.

But here—here was all of space before her. No one from their part of the galaxy had ever been here. This was like waking up in her very best dream. Some days Daphne Mandel had to pinch herself to make sure that she was really awake, and this was her job.

She hated having to interrupt it for anything. Sleeping and eating were minor necessities that she hadn't quite conquered yet, but given enough time she was certain she'd be able to overcome the need. So far, she had managed to grab food from the line in the galley and bring it up to her station; she really lost only about fifteen minutes a meal. Maybe twenty if someone moved too slowly.

The department was very small—*Voyager* had not been built as an outbound exploration vessel. But so far as Daphne Mandel was concerned, that meant there were fewer people to make mistakes.

Being unimportant meant they had a cramped suite in a back corridor, nowhere near any of the main functions of this ship. In Stellar Cartography were two large holotables where all the maps of the quadrant, old and new, could be displayed, compared, and refined. Sometimes the captain came down to look into the raw mapping to see the larger picture. More often, Cartography simplified the display and shrank it to two dimensions for navigation to display.

At one point in her Academy career, Mandel had been approached by her nav prof to consider a career move in navigation. She had scoffed at it. Nav was only about practical solutions where mathematial elegance was not properly appreciated.

No, Mandel had fallen in love with stellar cartography in her first year at the Academy and since that moment had resented any demands that took time away from her precious specialty. She couldn't waste minutes in social converstaion with her crewmates, let alone whole hours for social life and recreation. She resented the fact that her body required sleep. If she could, she would never ever leave her mapping station, not for a moment.

And now they were asking her for whole hours. And to work on something that was about to get them back. Well, all her work would be useless if it never got back to Federation space, even Mandel acknowledged that. But when she had realized that they were seventy years out, she had been ecstatic. An entire career mapping the unknown, capped by a triumphant return at the end.

And no dealing with her family, with all their anger and expectations and disappointments. She could forget about them forever. By the time *Voyager* had come home, they would all be dead.

No, she wasn't pleased to be assigned to work on a problem in Engineering, and she wasn't comfortable with the chief engineer. Torres was just like every other engineer Mandel had ever worked with, so much more concerned with tinkering and toys and making things run rather than appreciating the beauty of pure mathematics. In Stellar Cartography, even the computer program knew that this was the most exciting, rewarding work in the entire scope of Starfleet—one of the main reasons for Starfleet's existance.

That was something Mandel knew that no one in Engineering understood at all. She would bet money on it, if she had ever cared about money.

When she reported to Engineering, Torres was relieved to see her and didn't bother with preliminaries. "Look at this code and tell me why the computer isn't accepting navigational data," the chief engineer said.

Daphne Mandel looked at the screen. It was registering at point zero two percent. There was a lot of code there. She sighed and started. The sooner she finished here, the sooner she could return to her beloved stars.

"There is still some suspicion of tampering," Tuvok said evenly after Chakotay explained that the diagnostic had turned up nothing useful. "I would say that the fact that there was no easily identified evidence makes suspicion greater, not lesser. It is still highly unlikely that some being not from this ship, let alone our sector of the galaxy, could affect our computational system on that level. If there were a large-scale malfunction, it would be more likely our reception of whatever the dense datapack was. But something this fine is not the work of outsiders."

Chakotay said nothing. He wanted to contradict the Vulcan who stood before him, but he couldn't. The point was too clear. And yet, he knew that there was something else going on, something that he wasn't seeing. He was glad for the privacy the ready room afforded them. He could barely acknowledge the reality of such a theory himself. The crew would be affected. And if there were a saboteur aboard, that individual would be alerted.

"You may continue the investigation, Mr. Tuvok," Chakotay said. "But remember that we have no real evidence or suspects."

"I shall be discreet, sir," Tuvok said. Then the Vulcan left the first officer alone in the ready room.

There was no reason for sabotage here, Chakotay

thought angrily. They were all exiles. And no matter what their background or politics back home, they were united in a single quest to return. None of the rest of it mattered. Chakotay looked at the pad in his lap and rubbed his eyes in resignation.

The logical loop in all this was making him weary. Some coffee would have been nice. If they'd had any. Not that coffee would help clarify the problem. He'd have to rely upon the away team for that.

But somehow he thought that whatever they found would only make the problem bigger. That was the way it usually went. Something was very simple at the core, but discovering it empirically was often frustrating. He remembered an example from a children's book he had once read of a three-dimensional cone trying to explain itself to a two-dimensional plane.

Then again, who knew? he comforted himself. Maybe the away team had downloaded an entire alien archive that would explain it all in words of one syllable.

Nah, I wouldn't bet two credits on that one. Chakotay smiled. Probably a good thing that Tom Paris was on the away team.

CHAPTER
10

"THIS ISN'T WHERE WE CAME IN, CAPTAIN," KIM SAID, looking at the corridor they found themselves in.

"No, Mr. Kim, it certainly isn't. And that's probably a good thing," Janeway said, taking the lead, striding down the middle of the passage.

The hallway looked like nothing on *Voyager*. The bulkheads were curved, and there was no distinct joint between the walls and the ceiling or the floor. They all merged together in a rough ovoid. A few projections hung from the ceiling, and these were dark and dead. The whole felt like the interior of a rock cavern or an abandoned mine.

About halfway down they came to a darkened vestibule with a blank screen set well above their heads. The captain climbed the wall projections as if they were an elegant staircase back home. She turned her suit light on the screen. From the floor below, both Paris and Kim could see that it was a schematic of the ship. From this distance it was hard to make out what would have been the bridge and what was Engineering, or cargo, but that was less important than knowing where they were.

There was a single white dot amid the flat blues and oranges of the schematic. Presumably the dot represented the away team's current position. With the damage done to the hulk, even if the map had been easy to decipher, it would no longer match the present configuration. Still, Janeway was able to make a few educated guesses as to what was where.

The captain climbed down and selected one of the thick, flat nodes off the wall. She touched it and it opened into yet another cavernous hallway, this one looked just a bit brighter, busier, and better maintained than the one that had brought them to the holodeck. An entire series of flat amber projections glowed in a neat serpentine down one side of the floor. There were a lot more projections here. They looked like broken crystals, long and jagged with internal illumination in pink and pale green and a soft white that turned purple at the edges.

Several doors led off this passageway. Tom Paris assigned himself the point position and touched each of them gingerly. Two opened. The others were sealed with age and disuse, not intent.

The first area he explored was a small chamber

with only a few projections. He brushed his gloved fingers over the crystals. Only one or two glittered at his presence. He could make out nothing.

The other room was larger. He hadn't really looked in when he called the others to come see. Then he turned, and the area brightened, the colored ceiling crystals flickering in a manner he had almost begun to see as normal.

Suddenly, Janeway pointed to the center of the room and strode in that direction. In the center, on tatters of some kind of heavy patterned fabric, lay—a body. It was maybe four meters in length with six limbs arranged in death. The skin was grayish green in the odd light, but Janeway didn't know whether that was the alien's true skin color or if death had changed it.

She looked at its face for a moment, a face not at all humanoid but distinctly expressive. It had no hair at all, and its closed eyes were merely a slit. But for all that, Janeway thought she could see expression and intelligence in that visage. It reminded her of the dinosaur holograms she played with as a child, the ones in the basic math and reading programs with their warm, oversize claws and their bright cheerful smiles. Only this alien wasn't smiling. Its large lipless mouth must have smiled once and laughed, and there was something delicate and refined in the high bones in the cheeks and the definition of the jaw.

"Frozen. Too cold for even the internal bacteria to decompose the corpse. If there are internal bacteria," the captain said as she viewed the alien's remains.

"What killed it?" Tom Paris asked. "The cold? It looks like it was planned. I mean, it was just left lying here like this. And there aren't any marks on the body."

Harry Kim studied the tricorder. "I can't tell what killed it. I guess we'll have to hope the readings will be sufficient. Or we could take it back to *Voyager* with us, and The Doctor could do an autopsy."

"No, Mr. Kim. We don't know anything about these people or their funeral customs," the captain said firmly. "We'll get what we can from the tricorder."

Then she turned around and examined the room a little more closely.

While the bed with the deceased alien was the central focus, there were nooks and cubbies formed by the crystal projections in the walls and the ceiling. There were tatters of things left there, frozen. A few seemed to be remains of clothing. Two pieces seemed to be decorative, or at least Janeway couldn't figure any other purpose for their existence.

"Look, this must be a chair and desk."

Janeway joined him in the far corner and had to admit that the pillar formed by two projections was hollowed out in such a way that it looked like it could accommodate the bulk of the dead being on the bed. Well above the hollowed-out place a narrow shelf projected. That had to be what Harry thought was a desk.

To actually see it, Janeway had to climb up and stand in the hollow seat. There she could see the design clearly after Harry had finished recording it all.

Paris trotted over to the desk. "Hey wait," he said. "I think this has to be the computer. Lemme see." He touched the small pinnacles sticking up from the shelf, and several crystals lit up in pink and green and pale yellow. "Hey, did you try this? I think I turned it on."

Kim and Janeway stopped their own explorations. "You know," Paris went on, obviously excited, "I think that this might tie into the navigational system."

"And it might be the coffee machine," Kim said.

"Now *that* would be a discovery," the captain said.

They all laughed. Lightly, nervously, aware of the presence of death in the chamber.

"I've got it all on the tricorder," Kim said. "We can analyze it better with the facilities on *Voyager*."

Janeway nodded at the young ensign and started toward the exit of the death chamber. She walked so briskly that Paris and Kim had to jog to catch up with her. Not easy in the bulky suits with the projections on the floor and the faulty lights.

They seemed to be going upward. Without gravity functioning in the hulk, it was hard to tell, but

Paris thought that his ankles felt stiffer and were pushing forward the way they did in ski boots. The bootlocks kept him upright and moving, but the lack of weight didn't help any when it was so hard to move around!

"Maybe when we get to the controls we can turn on some life-support," he groused, mainly to himself.

"That would be excellent if you can locate the systems," Janeway said. "Of course, if you can locate the systems you'll know a great deal about their abilities and their entire operations center, which might be what we're dealing with here."

Paris nodded, forgetting that in the dark, in the suits, no one could tell. But the captain and Kim were ahead of him again, so he concentrated on sticking with them and not trying every door available. They were missing something by not doing a more thorough reconnaissance, he felt, but he also knew that they had limited time. They couldn't wander into every interesting side passage and study every room.

"This one," the captain announced with certainty. It was unlocked like the others, though when they went through, it wasn't to the place that Janeway had spotted from the shuttle.

That must have been an adjunct control room. This was the bridge. There was no mistaking it, Paris thought. Even if these people were incomprehensible in most ways by human standards, there was something about the bridge of a starship that defied differences in design. The pulse of residual power was still here.

The command chair was large and placed in the center, just as it was for the Federation and the Klingons, the Cardassians, the Romulans, even the Jem-Hadar. Here it was a polished fine crystal pillar that spanned the entire height of the structure, hollowed out as the chair in the death chamber had been, only with peaked control projections serrating the edges where one of the sets of limbs rested.

Directly opposite the command chair was the ubiquitous large screen display, now dead. Other stations dotted the walls surrounding the captain's post. They were much like the desk Tom had found so interesting earlier. The patterns of projections were different in each. He reached out a gloved finger but didn't touch this time. One of these was navigation, one was the conn, one was the helm. This was a starship. This was home.

"There aren't all that many variations on bridge designs," Paris heard himself say. "I'll bet that the helm and the conn are oriented toward the screen, and that life-support is somewhere in the back."

"What about weapons systems?" Kim asked, not looking up from getting every single station in the tricorder.

"This was a merchant ship, not military," the captain said. "Look at the cargo bays. Also, there aren't enough stations for a military ship. This was made to run with minimal crew."

Glancing around, Paris realized that the captain had noticed the essential immediately. It was true. There were only two forward positions, not three or four, and only two more positions on the back wall. Each of the console shelves was filled with projections. Maybe each unit served multiple purposes, so that even fewer people could actually run the ship than there were stations.

That would be terribly lonely, Paris thought. Such a huge ship with immense open space hauling gigantic cargos, and only five people on the bridge. Say they had three shifts, though there was no reason to assume that, Paris reminded himself. He was working within his own paradigm. Still, there was nothing wrong with the number three, either. It even made a great deal of sense for six-limbed creatures.

That would make a maximum of fifteen people aboard. Fifteen people. That wasn't many to spend months, maybe even years of a contract with. The isolation they must have felt . . .

Tom Paris shook himself as if to rid himself of a bad dream. Why was he thinking this way? He had always been much better at machines than people. This was not at all the way he generally approached a problem. Not even when a difference in culture and the misunderstanding was at the core.

The forward screen brightened and the image of

the indigo-skinned angel appeared again. The tree that had been burned by the phaser appeared intact. Although he knew it was a hologram, the picture disturbed him. There should be some sign that they had already been through that holodeck in person.

"Please help us," the hologram said. "We are in trouble and we will die if you do not come to our aid. We have been trapped here alone for longer than we can remember, and we are starting to lose our oxygen supply. Please help us repair our ship."

"They're transmitting that," Harry Kim said. "Like we had never even been there."

Paris glanced at the captain's face. Her mouth was set in a grim line, and her eyes were hard in the light of the transmission on the screen.

He'd seen that expression before. He never wanted to see that expression directed at him. She was angry, beyond angry, and she was going to do something about it. And the people who made her that angry were going to be very, very sorry.

Then Chakotay's face appeared in reply.

"That's strange," the captain muttered.

"Where is our captain and our away team?" the second in command demanded. "They came to help you, and they should be aboard your vessel now."

A tachyon burst filled the system with static. When it cleared they saw the holograms again.

"Why are they projecting this on their own

screens?" Paris wondered aloud. "It doesn't make any sense."

"Oh yes, it does, Mr. Paris," the captain said. "It makes a lot of sense if they know where we are. And given this little display, I'm fairly certain that someone is staging this whole show."

"And they're all holograms," Harry Kim said. "It reminds me of the Caretaker and the Array."

For a moment Paris's heart lifted. The idea that they might have found the Caretaker's companion, the only being they knew had the ability to send them home, was thrilling. And too good to be true, Paris told himself.

"No," the captain said. "The Caretaker created a hologram of things to put us at ease and created an environment that we could survive in. No, this is much less sophisticated. There are only casual similarities."

Something exploded in Tom Paris's brain. He could almost taste the answer, the sweetness of home. "It's like the Caretaker, but not quite up to specs," he said slowly, letting the words develop carefully as the ideas formed ferociously in his head. "Maybe whatever or whoever is doing this learned from the Caretaker's companion. Maybe the companion has come this way. Maybe somewhere in this computer there's a record of contact, of learning from this technological being that would set us on the right track."

Both the captain and Kim turned to him. "That

could be," Janeway agreed, sense fighting hope in her face. "Mr. Kim, can you download the computer log?" she asked briskly.

"I don't know, Captain," Harry said. "It would help if I knew how to access it, or what the log was, or even if they kept one."

"They kept one," the captain said with absolute conviction. "We just have to find it."

Chakotay was furious. He knew that no one else knew it, but he knew it. And he couldn't let whatever was broadcasting from that ship know it.

It was a trap. After they repeated their plea for help for the third time, when the captain and Paris and Kim were already over there, he knew for certain. It was a trap, and it was a bad trap to boot.

Chakotay knew that he had to get them out of there. No matter what these creatures were telling him, it was a lie. It had to be. They didn't acknowledge the away team, and Chakotay wished it was time for their check-in.

He tried their commbadges, but with the tachyon interference, the badges only reported an empty cackle. The fact that the away team couldn't be raised did not mean that they were in danger, Chakotay told himself. There were no life-sign readings on that alien vessel. There was nothing there to attack.

So why should there be a trap? What had put out the bait?

A trap was just a technique of hunting. Chakotay knew something about hunting. Some things wore different guises but never really changed. The hunter baits a trap and then waits for the prey to take the bait. The bait is different for different prey.

How could something in the Delta Quadrant bait a trap for mostly humans? How could it know that it wanted them? Or were there others here that it sought, and there was just enough similarity that this had all been meant for someone else?

But if that was the case, why was the language Federation Standard?

Chakotay was stunned when he realized it. Back home no one even thought of language as an issue. But here on the other side of the galaxy, they had been greeted in their own tongue. Fluently. Even poignantly.

How could anything without a Universal Translator use their language so quickly and so well? The Kazon and a few other races they had encountered seemed to have some translator capabilities, but the level of expression he had heard was not up to the same technology *Voyager* used regularly.

There was only one way it could be done so well. The alien computer must have uploaded their Universal Translator files.

That created a whole new set of questions. Chakotay wished he had some time to consider the larger implications, perhaps think through the puzzle.

But he didn't have the time.

He had a choice. He knew what the captain would do in his place. So he decided that he would have to do it himself not because it would make him feel better to take action than to order others to do so but because if the captain got angry about it, she would get angry at him.

CHAPTER

11

Kes showed up at the shuttlebay just as Chakotay arrived. "I'm coming with you," she told him, looking him straight in the eye.

"No, you are not," he corrected her. "You have duties in sickbay."

"I have duties here," she said. "If they are in trouble, they'll need medical assistance."

Chakotay weighed the advantages. Kes could be very useful if there was a need for her medical skills. If someone was hurt while they couldn't use the transporter, Kes might be able to keep him or her alive.

On the other hand, Kes was not a trained member of the crew, neither Federation nor Maquis. And given that she was fully half the medical personnel aboard, he thought risking her in an unplanned mission was not prudent.

But she was certainly brave.

Finally he nodded. "You know how to use an environmental suit?" he asked quickly. "It looks like there isn't much life-support left aboard the alien ship."

Kes nodded and smiled. She climbed into the shuttlecraft and belted down into the copilot's seat. She kept her medical kit on her lap.

"Clearance for shuttle," he spoke briskly into the board.

"Are you certain you wish to proceed with this, Commander?" Tuvok asked from the bridge. With both Janeway and Chakotay gone, the Vulcan was now the senior officer. "We do not yet know that the captain is in any danger."

"Just give me the all clear and lift the hatch," Chakotay ordered.

He had to protect his captain, his subordinates, maybe his friends. Even Tom Paris, who had been a Maquis for all of three weeks, and then only for the worst of reasons, was part of his tribe. His responsibility.

The indicator went green. Tuvok had obeyed and now the large bay doors were open to the dark. His fingers slid over the control panels, their bright yellow, green, red, and blue displays flashing. All the skills and pleasure he had in flying returned in a rush as he took the shuttle out of the bay and into space.

He tried to simply enjoy the flying. He had forgotten how he had missed it. His instructors were right, the skill never really did go away. There was a seventh sense for a pilot, a place where the mind merged with machine. Where there was no thought, but only being.

It was sacred space.

Kes sat quietly, almost like a statue, as he brought the shuttle around through the gash that Tom Paris had found so easy to navigate.

"There they are," he said, spotting the earlier shuttle already neatly parked on the exposed deck. "They would have had to wear environmental suits out there. There isn't any air in here."

"Are we going to stop next to them, or are we just going to call them?" Kes asked innocently.

Chakotay turned to her with absolute shock on his face. She was right! Inside this hulk there was no tachyon field. It was a null zone. And so his comm badge ought to work fine.

He flicked it on. "Away team, this is Chakotay. Where are you?"

"We're on the bridge trying to get a download from the alien log," Janeway's voice was crisp and clear. "How did you cut through the tachyon field? I thought our commbadges wouldn't work with the interference."

"Just a minor repositioning," Chakotay said, his voice perfectly calm. He ignored Kes's raised eyebrow and slight smile. "Do you have any idea when you'll be back aboard? We're getting a little worried."

"We're fine," the captain told him. "And I expect to be out of here in less than an hour. We'll have to do more investigation later, when we have a better idea of what we're looking for. We'll see you soon, *Voyager*. Janeway out."

"I suppose repositioning is an accurate way to describe it," Kes said as if she had learned something new. Her voice was so warm and soft, her eyes so innocent, it was easy to think she was human. The Doctor had been very impressed with her desire to learn, and now Chakotay knew why.

There was enough room to maneuver, to loop around through the blasted-out decks before emerging from the hole in the alien hull once again. Back into the tachyon field that somehow had never stopped its infernal buffeting and interference.

"No reason for them to know that we were out here, in case of an emergency," Chakotay said. "There was no emergency. But it's better to be prepared."

Kes agreed, her voice firm and serious.

Then suddenly she became still, and her body braced as if for some shock. "Something bad," she said, breathing raggedly. "Something bad is happening. Going to happen. I don't know. Get them out. Get them now." Her words became higher in pitch, her entire aspect growing more agitated as she strained against the shuttle belt.

Chakotay didn't hesitate. He flung the shuttle

into a blazing spin and whipped it out as they converged on the alien vessel again. As they approached the opening in the side, they were thrust backward by a force that nearly knocked Chakotay out of the pilot's seat.

Debris shot past them, piercing shards of the dead hull reeling out of control like a sandstorm around them, abrading the resistant skin of the craft.

Chakotay could not think. His mind was focused on one point, his entire being alive with a single purpose. To stay alive. To get through this bombardment of shrapnel.

He didn't remember putting the shields up, but the indicator light glowed on the console. Still, the shuttle shields were not complete protection against the discharge of junk that engulfed then.

He pulled the shuttlecraft hard to port, avoiding a tumbling chunk of metal blasted at them with the force of a projectile weapon. The shuttlecraft was awkward and bulky. It had not been designed for evasive exercises.

Kes gasped aloud. Chakotay ignored her. The first wave of wreckage had passed them now, but there were the smaller pieces that were traveling even faster and could tear right through their skin if it weren't for the shields.

They had shields, they had the shuttlecraft. The away team had nothing but the environmental suits, which had not been built to stand up to a frontal attack.

The captain, Paris, and Kim could be dead now. Chakotay felt it as a grim coldness that he ignored. No use imagining all the possibilities.

"They're alive," Kes said.

Chakotay heard her but didn't really listen. He had too much to do. Get back inside the dead ship while avoiding the leftover flotsam after the explosion. Find the away team and get them back. Get them safe, keep them alive.

This time it wasn't as easy to slip between the scarred plates of the dead ship. The force of the blast had loosened a tangle of internal wires and ducts that now hung like Spanish moss from every newly ripped surface. What had once been empty space was now a jungle thick with looping cables and masses of colored crystals caught in strands of mesh. Some of the crystals sparkled, and a few of the cables sputtered in the dark. Not everything aboard the alien craft was dead.

Chakotay cut power down to maneuver through the maze. "How are we going to find them in this mess?" he muttered to himself as his fingers flew over the console.

The commbadge should give me a good location reading, he thought. He had never wished so hard for a transporter on a shuttle. But wishing wouldn't do any good and the commbadge would.

He opened communications and tried to raise them. "Captain, Paris, Kim, what's your status?" he asked quickly.

There was no answer. The badge crackled empty

in the wake of the explosion. Fear tickled the back of his neck. If he couldn't find them, he couldn't save them. If they were alive.

They had to be alive. The commbadges were malfunctioning. Maybe they had been abraded by the dust of the explosion. Maybe they were shorted out in the environment. Maybe, maybe . . .

The clock was running. He tried the badge one more time. If he couldn't raise them, he could at least use the badges to trace them through the wreckage. Maybe they were unconscious or unable to talk.

Every second counted. "Away team, what's your status?" he asked again. His voice revealed no stress or concern. "Away team, we aren't getting any signal from you. Please identify."

"Chakotay? That you?" he heard Paris ask faintly.

"Yes. What's your status?" Chakotay demanded.

"I'm caught under a beam that's fallen. I can't see Harry or the captain."

"Okay, we'll get right on it," Chakotay said. He touched the console once more. This time it displayed a schematic of the local area with the three comm badges flashing red. That didn't necessarily mean that the badges were still on the officers, though given that they were wearing environmental suits, Chakotay would be very surprised if they had fallen off, unless a suit was ripped open. And then time wouldn't matter anymore.

He still had to steer through curtains of rubble to

get even close to the section where the indicators said that the away team had been trapped. When he reached the area there was no place to land the shuttle. It was too large and there was no surface left uncluttered by dangerously snaking live connections.

Chakotay took one look and grimaced. He was going to have to put on an environmental suit anyway. He used the magnetic locks to tether the shuttlecraft so that it remained tied next to a large, solid-looking projection.

When he was certain that the shuttle was secure and when he had a map of the interior of the area in his head, he turned to the back storage area to get the e-suit . . . and saw Kes, already suited, laying out the various pieces.

At least she hadn't put the helmet on yet. He had been so focused on finding the away team that he had forgotten Kes was there.

"Kes, what do you expect to do out there?" he asked. "There isn't anything you can do for anyone until we get them out of the suits and into a pressurized environment again."

"I can help you get them out of there," Kes replied.

"You're not strong enough," Chakotay waved her off. "Besides, your skills are more useful here."

Kes smiled sweetly. "But there's no gravity out there, so strength or weight don't matter. I can manipulate things as well as you can."

Chakotay blinked. The Ocampa lived underground. How could Kes have gotten any idea of the requirements of a zero-gee rescue?

He didn't have time to wonder. There was one door to the shuttle that was equipped as an airlock. Chakotay chose that exit and took Kes with him, for a single cycle.

The airlock cycled through and Chakotay grabbed at Kes so she wouldn't drift off when the door opened. His own boots were set on magnetic secured. Kes's boots were turned off. Chakotay suspected that she didn't know they could be activated. Now wasn't the time to tell her. He took her belt clip and attached it to a long strand on his own belt. That way they wouldn't get separated.

The airlock cycled through and the outer door opened.

Because his boots were on, Chakotay could walk out of the door and step onto the skin of the shuttlecraft. Kes floated behind, both her hands on the line that connected them.

They were in an alien world. Sheets of tubing and mesh cascaded around them like soft hanging art. Occasional flashes of hard white, or blue, or pale green light jumped between connections, backlighting the whole like an electrical storm. The crystals caught in the mesh sparkled on their own in softer colors than the flashes.

Chakotay had another long magnetic rope with him. It was fine filament and soft in his hands, but it ended in heavy magnetic disks to catch a steel object. Chakotay had never seen the thing used in real life for its intended purpose. People just thought of it as rope.

Now, secured to the hull of the shuttle, he began to swing the rope in a long lazy arc. There was no weight, there was no sensation of force in the rope as it looped around. Chakotay didn't let the feeling fool him. He aimed at a metal spike on the deck and threw, using the energy in the swing.

The magnet drew the rope end to the spike and it attached. Chakotay pulled at it hard, making sure it was fully secured. Only then did he turn his boots off and pull himself down the rope, heading away from the shuttle and deep into the alien wreckage.

It seemed that he was moving in slow motion through the vacuum. He had to be careful, couldn't afford to drift away from the tether or he and Kes would drift out into the hull, unable to return. Or they would drift right out the gash and into the tachyon field, where they would be bombarded, their suits abraded until they died. Quickly.

All these scenarios flashed through his mind as he made his way carefully to the interior of what remained of the vessel. Once there, he turned his boots back on and felt secure on the surface. He showed Kes how her boots worked so that he wouldn't have to keep her in tow. They had work to do.

There was no reason for talk as Chakotay led the way through the rubble. He knew where the away team was. Once there had been a bulkhead between him and the bridge. Now there was only debris, fragments of the wall still standing only because they were wedged there by other remains.

He took out his hand lamp and saw that Kes had turned hers on as well. He didn't know she'd brought one. It must have been in the medical bag.

Two lamps gave enough light that they could make out variation in the wreckage. Legs. Bloated shiny legs—those had to be legs in an environmental suit. It looked like half the wall had fallen on whoever was down there.

He couldn't hurry. He had to pick his way carefully through the ruins on the deck. It took less that half a second. It felt like eternity, seeing someone he knew down, hurt, trapped.

Maybe dead. He wouldn't think of dead. Only in need of help.

He couldn't see who it was at first. He was able to pitch the crystal from the chest area and look down. It was Harry Kim.

Kim was unconscious. Chakotay tried to dislodge the beam that had him wedged in, but it wouldn't move. The commander tried again, using all of his strength to push the single fragment that was either stone or metal or some odd combination of the two.

He looked to where the edge ended in a great heap that had crushed a station. This wasn't going to move. There was no matter of strength here, only the fact that the beam had nowhere to go.

Without thinking, Chakotay took the laser cutter from the pouch and cut the beam neatly. He was able to gauge it well, to get through the material without touching Kim's environmental suit. He smiled to himself.

"Kes, I need you over here now," Chakotay ordered the Ocampa.

"I've found the captain," Kes replied.

"How is she?" Chakotay asked as he slung his arm under Kim's back. At least without gravity and encased in the suit, he didn't have to worry that he could do further injury to the ensign. And without gravity, it was easy for him to carry Kim out of the rubble and back toward safety.

"I can't tell." Kes's reply came clearly through the helmet speakers. "She seems conscious but disoriented."

"Is she trapped?" Chakotay asked.

"No," Kes replied. "But I don't think she can walk."

"That's okay," Chakotay said. "See if you can carry her back to where we anchored. I've got Kim here. We'll get them back and then I'll go for Paris."

"No one has to go for Paris. Paris can do very well by himself." Tom Paris's voice came through clearly. "Just where are you?"

"Can't you see our lights?" Kes asked, worry coloring her tone.

"I see something that probably is you," Paris admitted. "But there are a lot of lights running around here. It's hard to tell."

"Okay, we'll wait and hold the lights steady,"

Chakotay said. "Follow them and join up with us, and we'll get you back to the shuttle."

"Good," Tom Paris said. "I can't wait to get out of this suit. How's Harry?"

"He's unconscious," Chakotay said. "Okay, I can see you now. We're at your two o'clock. And be careful of the junk on the deck."

Chakotay didn't really see Tom Paris. What he saw was a flicker of moving paleness against the dark.

Finally, the figure drew close enough that the basic humanoid shape, bloated by the environmental suit but still recognizable, was clear. Chakotay was pleased that no one could read his relief.

"Can you see us now, Tom?" Kes asked.

"Yes, I see you," Paris answered. "You've got the captain and Harry?"

"Yes," Kes reassured him. "But what about you? You're not walking well. Can you get across?"

"Like a stroll in the park," he answered, that cocky pilot's attitude returning.

But from the way he traversed the space remaining, Chakotay was not so certain that he was much better off than either of the other members of the away team. He listed heavily to one side and seemed off balance. If he and Kes hadn't been holding on to the captain and Kim, Chakotay would have insisted that Paris wait for aid. As it was, that wasn't possible.

At least without gravity it was easy to transport the injured. Chakotay cut the line that he had used to tie Kes to himself and used it to secure Kim and the captain to the magnetic line.

Chakotay had never thought he'd actually experience weightlessness in anything other than a controlled situation. He certainly never thought he'd be pleased about the situation. But given the possibilities, they would have had a much harder time in gravity.

The point was brought home trying to get the environmental suits off the captain and Kim. Paris wasn't going to be much help. He was moving too slowly, and Chakotay was certain that he was injured as well. But he would survive until they got him to sickbay and The Doctor.

The others were in worse shape. Taking off the suits had been harder than he had anticipated. He'd never unsuited someone who was unconscious or unable to help before. And Kes kept telling him not to move this way or not to pull that. Now that they were back in artificial gravity again, they had to follow all the procedures to guard against spinal column or nerve injury.

Or against making such injuries worse.

"Here, hold his shoulders while I get his legs," Kes directed him. "And keep him flat, whatever you do."

Chakotay followed her instructions and somehow they wrestled the suit off Kim without bending him or putting any pressure on his back.

"You two get the captain out of her suit," Kes directed. "I want to examine Harry."

This was a little easier. At least the captain was conscious. She was obviously hurt and unable to do much to help them, but she could move a little on her own, and they didn't have to worry about paralyzing her. But her eyes weren't focused and her words were fuzzy. Chakotay didn't understand what she was trying to say, and suddenly he was truly worried about her.

Chakotay wanted to do something for her. Now.

The only thing he could do was get her back to sickbay and fast.

The shuttle slammed hard to port. Before he could even yell, Tom Paris asked, "What is this thing secured with? A black hole?"

"We're tied down," Chakotay said. "And you're injured, you're not fit to fly."

"It's my leg that's hurt, not my head," Paris shot back. "You used the anchor?"

Chakotay slipped into the seat beside Paris who had taken the pilot's position. Chakotay didn't challenge him. Paris was an exceptional pilot. If he had any judgment left.

"Hurry," Kes said, her voice strained. "If we don't get Harry to sickbay soon he'll die."

CHAPTER
12

"HAVE YOU GOT A FIX ON THE CODE?" B'ELANNA Torres snapped at Ensign Mandel.

"I have isolated the problem segments," Daphne Mandel said softly, more as if she were analyzing the situation for herself rather than reporting to a superior. "I still have to go through all the code by hand and figure out not only what was wrong but how it was wrong and why. And who would have programmed it."

"Can you figure out who could have done it?" B'Elanna Torres asked, more interested than insistent. She was intrigued. She knew that people who were as good as Mandel could discover amazing things in code.

Ensign Mandel shrugged. "Depends. Different people have signatures writing code. It's like handwriting. You can tell if you've already seen a sample of it. But since there shouldn't be anything here that wasn't programmed by the original team, I should be able to figure out whose segment has the bugs."

B'Elanna Torres sighed. "Lots of people have written code since we left Deep Space Nine," the chief engineer explained. "The computer wasn't programmed for a lot of what we've encountered in the Delta Quadrant, and several people have had to patch things up fast. It isn't the best way, but at least we've gotten this far."

"You mean you just threw in quick fixes?" Mandel asked, her voice hushed with horror.

"We didn't have much choice," Torres replied curtly. "But each of them is dated and should be signed in the Engineering log. So you should be able to match them up fairly easily."

Mandel sighed deeply. "You know, it could be those patches that are creating the problem," she told the chief engineer. "Code that runs fine could trip up something farther down the line in another program when it gets put on-line. This could be something a programmer who wasn't careful enough created, trying to do a quick fix that would just get us through. Too many quick fixes just trip all over each other, and then you end up with a problem."

B'Elanna Torres paused for a moment and studied the ensign. Mandel was not being belligerent, she realized. The programmer appeared calm and rational and just a little bit tired. They were all tired.

"I hadn't considered that. You might be right," Torres agreed briskly. "If that's the problem, at least we'll know how to attack it from now on." Then the chief engineer smiled slowly. "If you're that good, we're going to have to get you transferred. Stellar Cartography is all very nice, but we can't afford this kind of problem even once. You'd probably make a great head programmer, and we could use one."

Daphne Mandel turned white. "Oh no, please, no," she whispered. But B'Elanna Torres had already walked away.

"Transporter, get a lock on the team and beam them directly to sickbay," Chakotay ordered.

"We can't tell who is who," the operator said.

"Then send everyone except the pilot to sickbay," Chakotay barked. He was angry. He was also worried. Kim's breathing had become ragged and uneven and his skin was cool. And he hadn't regained consciousness.

They were close enough to Voyager that the tachyon interference was not a problem. Signals didn't break up over such short distances.

"Can't you bring them in, sir?" the transport operator asked nervously. "I can't tell who the pilot is. And, uh . . ."

Chakotay remained calm, but it took all his self-control. The operator was pure Starfleet. In the

Maquis they had to be able to determine position and transport immediately with the wounded. He wished B'Elanna or even Tuvok were on the board now. Tuvok had served with his ship, albeit as a spy and for only a short time. But the Vulcan would have been able to transport the wounded and still leave someone flying the shuttle.

"How is he?" Chakotay asked Kes.

"It's very bad," Kes admitted.

If they weren't so close, he'd transport them all and abandon the shuttle. But now that wasn't an option. A wild shuttle could easily ram straight into *Voyager*.

There were no good solutions. Just try to get there faster. "Prepare an emergency respirator unit and ten cc's of impreferen and have them ready when we arrive," Kes added through her commbadge.

Paris pulled a perfect turn, arcing the shuttle so that it headed directly for the bay opening. There was not a wasted moment, not a single nanosecond that could be shaved off his flying. Even wounded, he was perfect. The commander's reverie was interrupted by a harsh choking sound.

Chakotay had heard that sound before. It was death. His body went ice cold. Harry Kim, young, innocent, dedicated Harry was dying.

"Come on, Harry, we're almost home," Kes said. Then she turned to Chakotay and Paris. "He's young and strong, and if the impreferen works, he'll recover," she reassured them.

"And what if it doesn't work?" Paris muttered through clenched teeth.

"Then The Doctor will know what to do," Kes said in a tone that brooked no argument.

Sweat ran down Tom Paris's brow. Chakotay knew that he and Kim were good friends. Paris was doing everything he could and then some to save Harry and the captain. But Tom had also been hurt, and the strain was starting to show.

Ahead of them the bay doors gaped black against *Voyager*'s silver skin. If pure will could move them faster, they would have hit warp. As it was, the shuttle glided seamlessly through the open portals and came to rest on the deck so gently that Chakotay couldn't feel the transition.

As soon as the Away Team materialized in sickbay, Captain Janeway staggered toward Harry Kim's bed. "How is he?" she asked, her own voice shaking with pain.

"He'll be fine," The Doctor reassured them. "If Kes hadn't acted promptly, it would have been much worse. But he's stabilized now, and in a few days he'll be as good as new."

Then The Doctor looked at the captain. "Which is not equally true of you. Up, up, here," he said, patting an examining table.

The captain sighed and sat gingerly. The Doctor made some noises as he looked at the medical tricorder readings. Then he turned to Kes. "Excellent. Your first diagnosis, absolutely flawless."

The captain cleared her throat. When that brought no response from The Doctor she spoke. "What diagnosis?" The Doctor looked at her and hesitated. "Well? Get this treatment under way. I can't spend all afternoon here." she snapped.

"I'm afraid you will have to spend slightly more than the afternoon, Captain," he said slowly. "You have a serious compression near the medulla oblongata and bleeding at at least three major junctures in the brain. The treatment for this will not take more than a day, but you will be required to stay absolutely still while the machines do their work."

"What?" the captain demanded, outraged. "You mean we can heal near death, we can force bones to knit in days, but you can't make a headache go away?"

"It isn't a headache," The Doctor began in his most pedantic manner. "You have several severe injuries that led to bleeding in the brain. Two hundred years ago this would have killed you in the next week or so. A hundred years ago you would have been crippled for life. I fail to see how a few hours under treatment to correct the situation is insufficient use of technology."

"I am the captain, we are in an emergency situation, and I cannot take a day to vegetate," Janeway said, furious.

"Captain, if you do not submit to treatment immediately, you will be unfit for duty. And as senior medical officer aboard, I will declare you unfit and relieve you of command. The choice is yours."

A look of absolute incredulity passed over Captain Janeway's face. "You wouldn't," she said.

"Oh, I definitely will, Captain," The Doctor said. "At the moment you are a danger to yourself and your judgment is impaired. You will be confined to sickbay until I approve your transfer."

The captain looked around. Even though her vision was fuzzy, she could not avoid acknowledging the scene. Around her, Chakotay, The Doctor, and Kes stood like guards, stone-faced and unyielding.

Only Tom Paris showed any sympathy. "Docs," he muttered to her. "They always want to keep you from having any fun. Made me stay out a whole week when I twisted my ankle once. They just don't understand."

The captain was obviously not amused. Nor was anyone else.

"It won't be long, Captain," Kes said. Under the soft, kind tone there was inflexibility. "Maybe not even a whole day if the affected areas are limited to what we found in the preliminary scans."

"Don't worry about the ship, Captain," Chakotay added. "We're under control here. I've got Mandel working with Torres on the code. We'll have the computer problem solved by the time you wake up."

"And the aliens?" Janeway asked weakly.

"They're less important than our own computer," Chakotay said. "And we've had enough casualties from that ship."

Janeway tried to nod and then pressed her hands to her ears. Her face went stark white.

The Doctor came around and put a supporting arm across her shoulders. "Some problem with balance is not unexpected at this point," he said, easing her down.

The hypospray appeared in his hand as if by magic. He injected the captain before she realized anything had happened. "What?" she started to ask. But then she fell asleep before she could finish her question.

"A few hours of sleep with that, and you'll be good as new," The Doctor promised her sleeping form. "Well, maybe not as new, but at least functional."

He turned away, satisfaction glowing from his face.

"You know, you could get written up for insubordination, Doc," Paris said.

"When the captain is better, I think she will agree that The Doctor had no choice," Chakotay intervened. "Now let's let the sick get better and the rest of us get to work."

"You're fit for duty, Lieutenant Paris," The Doctor said. "Just don't do anything stupid, like that skiing program."

"It is not stupid," Paris said as Chakotay escorted him out of sickbay. "Skiing is a great sport."

He was already gone and the door closed behind him before The Doctor shook his head in negation. The he turned to Kes, who stood next to Harry Kim's bed. "You did an excellent job here, Kes," he said. "It was fortunate that you went. He might not have survived otherwise."

Kes smiled softly.

"Shouldn't we check on Harry?" she asked. She didn't wait for an answer but turned away and studied the readings on the display.

"I said it was very fortunate that you went," The Doctor said, joining her. "But how did you decide to go? How did you even know that the commander was leaving the ship? I find this rather uncanny."

Kes looked at her hands. "I don't know how I knew. Or why. I only felt that I should go, and there was Chakotay with the shuttle. Like it had been set up."

"Set up," The Doctor repeated. "Hmmmm. Now if you were Betazoid, I would know there was some empathic being behind this. But you're not. And you don't want to be tested."

"Right now we both have better things to do."

She turned away and immediately went to the captain's side as if there were something necessary for her to do there. The Doctor didn't pursue her, and she was glad.

"How could it be set up?" Kes asked the sleeping form of the captain. "How could that be and I wouldn't even know it?" Then she paused and thought about how unlikely all the coincidences seemed. "How could it not have been set up?" she asked softly. "Almost as if that explosion was planned and someone wanted to make sure that medical care was there. As if we were sent in as a rescue team."

She turned the idea over in her mind, and the more she looked at it, the more it made sense. Even though The Doctor hadn't bothered teaching her statistics yet, she realized just how unlikely the set of coincidences was.

She saw it, and it frightened her.

CHAPTER
13

THE BRIDGE OF *VOYAGER* WAS NOT A GOOD PLACE TO try to dissect what was happening, Chakotay decided. He needed to glance over to his left where he could see the controls of the helm glowing as if they were perfectly functional. Behind him Tuvok had a nearly whispered conversation with someone Chakotay could not immediately recognize. He heard footsteps and then the slight whoosh as the turbolift opened, and he wondered what the conference was about.

Chakotay still could not help but speculate about what had prompted his own intuition to rush off to the alien ship.

He had thought that the idea of going over and checking on the away team was his own. But something else nagged at his awareness. *Voyager*. He would not leave the ship without leadership. He knew his duty, and he knew the captain. Why had be become so concerned *before* they had missed their check-in?

That was not like him, Chakotay realized.

And then the explosion right as he and Kes were ready to leave, as if the whole thing had been timed to make certain that no one was hurt. That rescue was there at the moment.

"Commander, we need authorization for a diagnostic on the holodeck."

Chakotay glanced up to the face of a young ensign in gold. "Is there a problem with the holodeck?" he asked.

"No, sir. It's routine maintainence."

Chakotay sighed and pressed his thumb to the pad the junior engineering officer presented to him. Then he updated the log, speaking softly so as not to distract the bridge crew working around him.

He returned to his analysis, wondering wryly what Tuvok would think. The Vulcan was just behind him on the bridge, and Chakotay knew that he wasn't observing the bridge at all. No, Tuvok's eyes would be glued to his monitors, his hands resting gently on the edge of the control pad ready to bring up the shields or target phasers if it came to that. So far it hadn't.

The more he considered the subject of sabotage,

the more disturbed he became. He didn't like the idea of some alien being manipulating his judgment. It felt—Cardassian.

That was absurd. There were no Cardassians in the Delta Quadrant. And there were plenty of other aggressive races like the Kazon, all too hopeful of either acquiring *Voyager*'s technology or destroying it.

But the Kazon didn't admire sneaks and sabotage. They did their killing in the open, if his experience with the Ogla was carried over to the other sects. So far, of the many cultures they had encountered in the Delta Quadrant he had not found one yet that seemed to enjoy subterfuge as much as the Cardassians.

Maybe Tuvok was right, there was a saboteur aboard, and there was nothing at all odd about this collection of junk and tachyons that now filled the large forward screen. A twisted piece of dark metal floated by so close to their sensors that Chakotay could make out orange images that had been worn to shadows on a broken curved beam. A tail of bright wires was attached in a clump that Chakotay thought looked like a jellyfish. The whole tumbled once, and then there was only the giant hulk they had explored left alone on the screen. From this distance the gash they had entered looked like a dark line painted down the side, something neat and decorative.

It was easier to think of a spy than the alternative. At least that made sense. It fit into his world-view, and things behaved in a reasonable and predictable way.

Spies were known to exist. But they had taken no new crew aboard since leaving the Alpha Quadrant, except for Kes and Neelix. Chakotay tried to imagine either of them as spies. Both, he knew, had had dealings with the Kazon. And Neelix had been in contact with many local races.

He could not really see either of them as saboteurs. Neither had the technical expertise, though his observation of Kes told him that she was well able to have acquired it, should she have desired. But all her time and energy had been consumed by learning medicine, and there was no indication that she had ever accessed any technical data on *Voyager*'s computer system.

Which left an invisible entity or someone who had been aboard since the Alpha Quadrant. And any spy who had come aboard in the original crew was more likely Cardassian than any of the other antagonistic races he knew from home.

To his right he noticed a sudden movement. Two crew members, one in blue, were consulting the monitors there. He turned, but from his vantage point could see no discernible difference. If it were anything important, they would report to him immediately.

But they stood, one with her head slightly tilted to one side. Then she identified something and touched a green semicircle, drawing her finger toward the yellow. She nodded and returned to another station while the original observer appeared satisfied.

Chakotay returned to his ruminations. Members of the Obsidian Order had no qualms about mental control, if they were able to exercise such. And there were rumors that the Obsidian Order indeed did have some experimental success with empathic control.

It even made sense that it would work on Kes and on himself. Kes seemed to have some empathic gifts, though precisely what and how they worked were unknown. As for himself, he was not an empath. But his strong spiritual upbringing and nature had taught him to be more attuned to the spirit worlds. And he was certain that any psi abilities in any race worked on the spirit level. After all, wouldn't human shamans and healers test high positive in one or several of the psychic ranges?

He wished that there had been a counselor aboard with the expertise to identify possible psionics.

True he had some small ability, enough that he was able to perform basic rituals. A small ability. Not trained, and therefore vulnerable to a great ability.

The loneliness he had felt, and the compulsion to find the away team when he should have stayed on the bridge. These were not his feelings then. They had come from elsewhere, and served some purpose that was not his.

He wanted to discuss this with Kes. Maybe she felt the same way. Maybe her gift was larger than his or different, so that she had a clearer perception of who could be responsible. Maybe she could help him track down the traitor.

He decided to wait until the captain had taken command, until Kes was off duty in sickbay. She was needed there.

Meanwhile, however, he needed to talk with Tuvok. The Vulcan never had abandoned the notion of sabotage. Now Chakotay had a little more insight into how it was done, which would mean that they might be able to narrow down the field enough to find a Cardassian. Before someone else was hurt. Or killed.

Before he could even move discreetly over to the security officer, B'Elanna Torres burst onto the bridge and demanded his immediate attention.

"I can't work with her," Torres said loudly enough that no one could help overhearing. "It's impossible. She's impossible. She wants to take everything so slowly, and we don't have that kind of time."

Chakotay spoke to her softly. "I think we should talk in private."

B'Elanna glowered for a second and then realized what she had done and colored. "Yes, sir," she said meekly, and followed Chakotay to the ready room. Once the door was decently shut behind them she started again. "It's that Ensign Mandel. You'd think I was asking for fine art or something. I am sick of her criticizing the way we've done everything. As if we created the problem in the first place, not programming as prettily as she might like. Well, if she wants everything so neat and careful, maybe she should come down and change specs in the middle of an emergency. Why can't Harry come and do some of this? At least he understands what we need."

Chakotay waited a moment for her to calm down. Once she regained her composure, she was able to see solutions no one else could have imagined.

"Let's take it from the beginning," he said as her breathing returned to normal and she sat heavily in a chair. "First of all, I don't know if you've heard. Harry was injured on the away team. He'll be better soon, but he's in sickbay for the time being."

"Harry's hurt?" Torres asked, her entire concern suddenly shifted to Kim. They'd worked together a good bit, Chakotay realized. And they made a good team.

"He's going to be okay," the exec reassured her. "But he's got to remain under treatment and observation for a couple of days."

"Can I see him?" B'Elanna asked quickly.

"I think they've got their hands full for the moment," Chakotay said. "And I think you've got your hands full, too. The Doctor and Kes will take care of Harry. You've got to take care of the computer, and I don't think I need to tell you which is the more seriously injured of the two."

B'Elanna sighed heavily. "Yes. I get it. But that Mandel creature, she's impossible."

"What is she doing, precisely?"

"She's taking way too much time with all the details."

"Why do you think it's so out of line?" Chakotay asked softly.

Torres looked at the ceiling and bit her lip. Long moments of silence passed as she reviewed the data. Then she looked back at Chakotay. "The only times we've touched any of the navigation programs has been for the star charts. Her star charts. Most of what we have done has been in ship's systems, especially power sharing. Trying to get a little more for the replicators, basically. Sometimes the shields. But those are peripheral systems, and you know that they're discrete in the architecture."

"No," Chakotay said. "I didn't know that. Computers are not my field of expertise, and *Voyager*'s system is a couple of generations more sophisticated than what I learned to work with anyway. How much interaction between subroutines is there?"

Torres blinked. "None. Or almost none. The thing is, the more I look at it, the more I am certain that the patching we've done couldn't have affected the navigational systems and especially couldn't have done anything to the base connections. That's the first level of recognition. Whatever changes happened, they were right at the center of our programming and they affected things as basic as breathing."

Chakotay nodded. He followed that much. "So you're saying that you don't believe this could be an accident and that she's wasting time looking at an improbable scenario?"

"That's it. Exactly," B'Elanna got up and leaned her hands on the table. "I can't tell whether she's doing this on purpose because she wants to be back up in Stellar Cartography, or whether she just doesn't have any idea of what the word urgent means. You would think she'd be happy to stay here for the rest of her life and never get home. Let alone to the next food and fuel stop."

Chakotay froze in thought for a moment. He had wondered about a Cardassian spy, and here was someone vital to their needs who was making life difficult. It fit. It fit far too neatly.

He wanted to confide in Torres, to get her reaction to his suspicions. He didn't. He knew he could be wrong, and he didn't want to prejudice her. If Mandel was reliable, they needed her skills. More than ever now that Harry was incapacitated. Daphne Mandel was a first-rate programmer, at least according to her records.

And what if those records had been forged? Chakotay had no illusions about security against the Obsidian Order. If they wanted to create a false background, even one that included Starfleet Academy, they could do it.

"Get back to work," he said heavily. "Tell Mandel to look at the transmission from the aliens before getting more involved in other programming fixes, and you can tell her that's a direct order. If she has a problem with that, she should come to me, not you."

Torres looked at him with growing comprehension. "There's something else going on here," she said slowly. "And you're not telling me."

Chakotay smiled. "I'm not telling you because I'm not sure if anything is going on. But tell Tuvok I want to see him when you leave."

B'Elanna's look was pure speculation as she left. Chakotay regretted that he couldn't let her in on his suspicion. But she was going to be working with Mandel, and B'Elanna Torres was not capable of hiding her feelings. If she suspected Mandel was a saboteur, the programmer would know it in two seconds flat. That wasn't the way to catch a spy.

He missed having B'Elanna's input, though. When they had been fighting the Cardassians together, she had been almost as valuable for her assessment of a situation or a Cardassian tactic as she had been for her engineering talents.

She understood their engines, their mechanics, their programming almost as well as she understood her own. And that gave her some insight into what they could do and how they thought about tactics. It also meant that she might be able to identify a Cardassian writing code, even in their own language for their own computer. A signature.

She could have identified it better than anyone. Certainly better than Harry Kim, who had never fought them. Harry had graduated from the Academy after the final peace accords, and all the classes in the world and all the history of the various Cardassian conflicts wouldn't teach him the quirks and turns of mind that would show up in a computer.

"You wished to speak with me, Commander?"

Tuvok's arrival broke into his wool gathering. "Sit down, Commander," Chakotay said. "We discussed the possibility of sabotage earlier, and you were planning to continue your investigation. Have you found anything yet?"

"Nothing decisive. However, the circumstances are most indicative of some untoward activity originating here."

Chakotay nodded. "I may have a lead for you," he said, and then he proceeded to tell the security officer about Torres's reaction to Daphne Mandel.

"What makes you suspect a Cardassian agent under deep cover?" Tuvok asked, curiosity making him sound almost as if there were emotion behind the question.

Chakotay cleared his throat. He didn't quite know how to explain the uncanny feelings he'd been having lately. Faced with the Vulcan's pure logic and patience, he suddenly thought that his recitation sounded thin and ephemeral.

Tuvok, however, did not react negatively. "So you say, Commander, that you believe that you and

Kes have experienced some manipulation from a trained empath or telepath who is sending messages. However, it appears that Lieutenant Mandel could have had no knowledge of the away team's problems or your plans."

"Then you think it unlikely that Mandel is a problem?" Chakotay asked.

Tuvok remain absolutely still. "I did not say that, Commander. In fact, I think that you may have given me a very valuable lead, and I shall pursue it as soon as I leave this office. However, from your description of events, I think it is possible that there are two entities involved and only one is Cardassian. It is my belief that something is happening with the aliens here and that our Cardassian saboteur is merely taking advantage of the opportunities."

"Every time I think we're getting closer to a solution, the mess only gets worse," Chakotay said. "We were looking for one saboteur. Now we've got two entities. And two injured."

"I shall begin with Ensign Mandel immediately," Tuvok returned to the task at hand.

Chakotay shook his head. "I've asked Ms. Torres to order her to inspect the computer logs during the time frame of the alien transmission, instead of concentrating on all the programming anyone has done since *Voyager* left home port. I think that her reaction to being assigned a very specific task might push her to reveal herself."

"An excellent plan, Commander," Tuvok congratulated him. "However, if the computer problems originate with the aliens, it may well be to her benefit to bring it to our attention, thus throwing any suspicion from herself."

"If she recognizes an alien pattern and corrects the program, then we can deal with her being a spy later. If she is one. I don't want to make assumptions too easily."

"Understood," Tuvok said. "I shall be discreet. But we will discover a solution."

"And we'd better do it quickly," Chakotay added. "We've already had injuries, and we've lost two days out of our schedule."

"Schedule?" Tuvok asked. "Why would that take precedence over the current situation?"

Chakotay sighed. He had known why Janeway was so careful about timing, but having looked into the supply situation himself, he had been horrified by how few reserves *Voyager* had.

"Yes, schedule," Chakotay said. "This region of space is fairly empty. It will be at least two weeks before we hit the next M-class planet where we can resupply. Our stores are very low, Mr. Tuvok. That is not for general knowledge. But if we can't get away from here in the next two days, we risk shortages and food rationing. I don't have to tell you what that would mean."

"Being required to eat less of Neelix's cooking is a dubious hardship," the Vulcan said.

"I think a lot of us would agree with you,"

Chakotay said, smiling. "But we need food. And we need supplies, and we're not going to find anything out here until we get to the next star system, which is two weeks away at our current safest speed. And that means we can't linger here and indulge our curiosity. There isn't any good reason for us to be here except that we're trapped by a malfunctioning computer that won't let us go anywhere else."

"I appreciate the gravity of the situation," Tuvok assured Chakotay. "And I shall pursue this Ensign Daphne Mandel discreetly. I, too, have no reason to wish to stay in the middle of this wasteland. We shall resolve the problems very quickly."

Tuvok left and Chakotay was alone. "I wish I was as confident as you are," the commander muttered at the closed door.

Ensign Mandel was aghast. "I thought you wanted me because I know what I'm doing," she protested. "Now you're telling me to take a completely different course of action and trash what I've just done when it could lead to an answer."

"This could lead to an answer, too," B'Elanna Torres said. "And it's a direct order from the commander. So if you have a problem with it, you can take it up with him."

"He doesn't know nearly enough about programming," Mandel explained didactically. "It's much more likely a malfunction, bits of code tripping over each other, than it is some alien transmission.

How would some alien know anything about how our computer works, anyway? Let alone be able to reprogram it on this deep a level. It doesn't make sense."

"If you have a problem you can take it up with the commander," B'Elanna repeated herself, then walked away leaving Mandel shaking her head in utter disbelief.

Daphne Mandel slowly looked away from the screen where she had been reviewing the alterations that had been made in *Voyager's* computer code since they had entered the Delta Quadrant. She had already cleaned up a good bit of what she had studied. Her changes might even save a touch of energy or speed a process. She was very pleased with her work. It was fun, rewarding. Maybe not quite as much fun as stellar cartography, but fun all the same.

And she had felt almost as if she were part of *Voyager*. That element of her personality, her perception, was now integrated into the fabric of the ship.

She knew that what the commander wanted surveyed wouldn't take long. But she had been doing so well with the other job, and this was probably a dead end. And then she would find out that the whole problem was not an alien communication at all but that the power and frequency that the communication came on had burned out an essential line or two or garbled some subroutine. It would turn out to be something boring, and then she wouldn't get to finish the fine-tuning that needed to be done.

But it was a direct order. To disobey, even when she was certain she knew better, would be insubordination. Daphne Mandel was no rebel. She liked order, she liked the security in the chain of command. Sometimes that meant doing something she didn't like because someone in authority had ordered it. And she believed in orders to the very depths of her soul.

Very slowly she moved to blank the screen. Then she called up the internal logs for the specified time. At this level the screen filled with what appeared to be a jumble of meaningless garbage.

To Daphne Mandel it was perfectly comprehensible. As she stared at it, she was able to start seeing patterns, traces that flowed through the routine business of the day. She went back ten minutes to get a view of the internal workings before the alien transmission so that she could separate what was alien and what was *Voyager*.

She didn't read and translate line by line. Instead she became passive, let her base mind get into this mode of thought. She was actually thinking in machine language, naturally and without interpretation.

Her concentration was so profound, she was almost in a trance. Nothing existed except bytes and movement. She started recognizing the bio-packet components, which had four instead of two possible positions for storing data and their parallel architecture. She began to understand the map of the internal universe of the computer in the same way she understood the map of the stars.

It was nothing she could explain. Rather it was like a dream; she could feel it and had a sense of where the next place was, what the next lead meant. But to try to categorize it in human language would kill the fragile structure of her knowledge.

"Excuse me, Ensign Mandel. Could I be of any assistance to you?"

The voice broke into her trance and destroyed her train of thought. The symbols, which only a second earlier had begun to resolve into something greater, went flat and meaningless again. She whipped around in her chair to see who had broken her concentration at that crucial point.

A close-faced Vulcan looked back at her, his expression no more than mildly curious. "I did do some studies in Computer Architecture," he said blandly. "And Commander Chakotay has informed me that this is currently the highest priority project aboard. He said that everyone who could be of assistance should consider this to override all normal functions and duties. Therefore, I have come to offer my assistance."

Daphne Mandel blinked. She tried, truly she tried, not to want to kill him. She had been so close, so very near the heart of the problem. Just a little longer and she would have seen it all clearly.

Suddenly she understood B'Elanna Torres's temper. It wasn't simply a Klingon thing. It was the inevitable frustration of having to deal with people who did things wrong, who made stupid mistakes, who interrupted in the middle of delicate intellectual processing.

That didn't happen in Stellar Cartography. People left her alone. She realized that was a luxury most of the crew on *Voyager* didn't have. Especially the chief engineer.

But unlike B'Elanna Torres, she had not been working for months on keeping her temper in check. Daphne Mandel didn't even know she had a temper. Not until Lieutenant Commander Tuvok destroyed the ethereal mental construct she needed in order to do her job.

"No, I don't need your assistance, sir," she said furiously. "All I need is to be left alone." She turned away from him, barely able to leash her combined anger and confusion. He was a Vulcan. Didn't he understand that interruption was the worst thing anyone could do to the fine art process of programming?

"That is not logical," Tuvok pointed out. "The problem is one of proportion, and the more people working on it, the easier is the burden."

"Logic be damned; it isn't a logical process," Daphne Mandel sputtered, completely baffled. No reasonable person could think that she had been involved in anything but the finest creative endeavor. "I was *in there,* and it's going to take a long time to recreate that, and you went and blew it. Right out of the water. I would have had it in twenty minutes, another hour. I would have *had it*. It is art, and it was going to be perfect, and you ruined it."

"I do not understand the process you are trying to describe," Tuvok said.

"You don't understand? Well, I don't care what you understand or don't understand. Do Vulcans even have art? How can you create a perfect program and not understand?"

She stared at him for a moment, waiting for an answer. The Vulcan said nothing, and that perplexed Mandel even more. "I'm going to my quarters. No one is going to disturb me there."

Daphne Mandel got up and strode angrily to the turbolift. Tuvok let her go.

CHAPTER
14

THE SECURITY OFFICER DID NOT RETURN DIRECTLY TO his station on the bridge. Instead he went to a lesser station in the security office, with a board that included readings on every area of the ship. It was staffed by an ensign, who was trying to remain alert. Tuvok had some sympathy for the boy. The job was detailed and dull and nothing ever happened.

Except now.

"When Ensign Mandel returns to her quarters, lock her in," Tuvok ordered the officer at the board.

A good security recruit, all he replied was, "Yes, sir." And showed no curiosity about the order, either. Tuvok didn't know whether to think that was reassuring or worrisome.

He didn't have time to concern himself with it,

though. That suitability of the boy to the position was a minor consideration in even placid times. Right now there were much more important things that needed investigation.

Daphne Mandel's reaction to his very benign offer indicated that she was not trustworthy. Not given the present conditions. Then Tuvok reported to the bridge to tell the executive officer what he had done.

Daphne Mandel didn't know she had been sealed in her quarters, that she was essentially under arrest. If she had known, she wouldn't have cared. In fact, she would have been very pleased to know that no one was going to disturb her, which was why she had left Engineering anyway.

It was a glorious luxury to be all alone with her work, in the comfort of her own space. She had a big armchair full of cushions and a soft flannel throw that she wrapped around her shoulders. There were no distracting people or lights here, only her nice familiar paintings.

"Computer, transfer data from work station E-51 to this terminal," she said. The computer most likely did not note the pleasure in her voice and the ease with which she sprawled in the chair.

Now she would be able to get something accomplished.

The computer transferred the data with no trouble. That in itself was indicative. Either the malfunctions were tied up with a single program, or the computer considered her requests valid and non-threatening.

That made Daphne think about the center of the computer itself. Because even in the bare glimpse inside she had formed—not quite a theory. Theory was far too grand a word. More a hunch, a vague idea of the computer as personality.

In assessing people of whatever species, the mind processed a large number of unquantifiable details to arrive at a single reaction. She had had more than a passing interest in this when she was a cadet, even more so since Dr. Vhanqz was one of the team creating the high level biocomputers. His team had spent years researching sentient processing and how this influenced personality and reaction. So she knew that she had been trained all her life to judge things like appearance and body language and vocal tone and pupil dilation to make her assessment.

The computer had none of these tools, let alone the subtle training that said *This face is not trustworthy* or *This is someone I really want to know.* The whys of such a decision, Dr. Vhanqz taught, were based on immediate recognition of hundreds of subtle clues, all of them processed together.

The fact that all the information was parallel helped decision making. And when he created his first biocomputer with high recognition capabilities, he had used a crude form of this kind of parallel reasoning. Dr. Vhanqz's machine was the prototype for *Voyager's* computer. So Daphne knew that this computer possessed a certain level of what could only be called judgment, which was one of the reasons why she had wanted to check the fixes.

These people were used to working on computers that didn't do integrated processing of this nature. They would have regarded their additions and jury-rigs as peripheral when in fact the computer on *Voyager* had the ability to use this data as indicative of other problems.

Mandel was convinced that the computer had an idea of what was going wrong with *Voyager*. It must know that they were lost, and it must be trying to fix that. How, precisely, she didn't know yet. And why it had stopped all of a sudden here, now, was not clear to her. But she would bet real money that it had something to do with the alien transmission.

The alien had told *Voyager* something. She just had to get in and find out what it was.

She began to fall back into the trance of deep concentration once more, this time slowly as if a light shone through a gauze curtain in her mind.

She lost track of time, of herself entirely. There was only interaction, the computer responding to instruction. There was order and precision in this place.

And then there was a message. It was clear and in her own language, and it was strange and lonely. Daphne Mandel did not understand completely, but she could comprehend intuitively what it was. She knew. This time she really knew.

She had to tell someone. Chakotay or B'Elanna Torres, someone who would understand. Not Tuvok.

She went to the door of her quarters, her mind barely registering the physical realities. She was still far too deeply entranced in the revelations of the code. She walked straight at the door and straight into it.

The door didn't open. She tried again, and again it locked her in. There was no reason to this, she thought. Maybe this was all a dream and she was trapped, trying to get awake. That made as much sense.

She tried to leave one more time. Now she was certain that she had been locked in.

The computer. She knew the secret, she knew the aliens. And it wasn't going to let her tell.

Daphne Mandel wondered how long this would last. She wondered if the computer meant to starve her here, or let her die of thirst. Her replicator rations were low anyway.

But they would come for her. She knew that. They wouldn't let the computer hold her prisoner the way it was holding *Voyager*. The way it had been told.

Voyager's computer didn't understand that the aliens were going to starve *Voyager* to death. The computer, for all it had judgment and intelligence, was innocent. It had no program to recognize evil. It had no concept of ill intent.

And the alien who had sent the transmission was

using that. It had begged for help, for company. Begged? Not precisely, Mandel thought. Ordered was more like it. It had inserted instructions to stay in the deepest levels of the computer's program.

Now she had to get that out. Only she couldn't do it from her own terminal. She had already tried and the access was restricted, which only made sense. In fact, she was almost relieved to find at least some safeguards still in place.

No, she had to get down to one of the main programming stations in Engineering, much as she didn't like either the department or the chief running it. And then she had to tell the captain. Maybe Tuvok and Torres as well, but the captain was the one who needed to know most of all.

The captain could do something even while she was locked in, Daphne Mandel thought. The captain could have someone else get started on the basics of disassembling the problematic code while someone else distracted the locking routines. It was the best Daphne could think of on short notice.

She tapped the comm switch on her terminal and requested the bridge. "You are not cleared for that request," the computer informed her.

Daphne was stunned. She thought about it, and that did make sense. She wasn't bridge staff, she wasn't a senior officer. She spent her time holed up as far from those centers of activity as she could get.

She curled up in her big overstuffed Andorian chair, the one luxury item in her quarters. It was her thinking place, her working place where her body was utterly comfortable so her mind could be free. Now the comforting hollows of the great chair cradled her, and the unutterably soft Andorian cashmere caressed her exposed skin.

And so she could find a solution. She knew she could.

Perfectly, utterly confident and calm, she reviewed the goal. She was here, she had to transmit to over there, and the computer was in the way. She breathed deeply, the near trance she had needed in order to read the computer code settling on her once again.

"If you will wait one more minute while I run this final scan, you will be free to go," The Doctor tempted Captain Janeway.

Who, in all honesty, did try to comply. The Doctor was right to be thorough, she told herself again. No matter how well she felt, she couldn't risk the possibility that there was something the basic pressure to the base of the brain and nerve stem was masking. A buildup of internal fluid pressing on the brain that could cause changes in perception and even personality was possible. The Doctor had told her about that in grim detail.

"The way our luck has been running lately, I wouldn't want to take the chance," she had agreed. And so she endured these infernal tests while she should be on the bridge.

Not that there was anything she could do, she

told herself. B'Elanna and the programmer and Tuvok were the ones who had the essential skills to pull them through. And Harry Kim still lay sleeping in the restorative restriction of a reconstruction unit.

"When will he be ready to come back on duty?" she asked Kes as The Doctor studied the output of the latest scan.

"Very soon," Kes said, reassuringly. "He's healing very quickly. Exceptionally well, really. Maybe six or ten more hours, and he'll be as good as new again."

"Youth," the captain sighed, and smiled. "So, what about me, Doctor? Fit for duty?"

The Doctor began to clear his throat when the communications speaker came through with the dispassionate computer voice. "There is a medical emergency report from Quarters Two-Zero-Three Alpha on restriction."

"Go ahead," The Doctor barked.

"This is a restricted terminal on security alert," the computer continued.

"This is a medical emergency," The Doctor said. "Put it through immediately."

"Doctor, this is Daphne Mandel. I have to get a message through to the captain."

"What is the nature of the medical emergency?" The Doctor snapped.

"I have isolated the alien transmission," Daphne's voice sounded clearly over the speaker. "But I can't reconfigure the program from my quarters. And I seem to be locked in. Anyway, I've found it and we can delete it and get away from here. This is some kind of alien—I don't know what—a thing to make us stay here. And it's inserted right into the code of the basic operating system. Can you tell the captain that? Someone else will have to get down and pull it all out, but I have the locations."

"You've just told the captain," Janeway said. "Why are you restricted?"

"I don't know," Mandel replied. "I think maybe the computer knows what I'm doing. I can't think of anything else. But I'll start relaying the line numbers that have to be deleted now, and anyone can change them that way. It should be very easy."

"Excellent," the captain replied.

And then the computer cut in. "This is not a medical emergency discussion. Vocabulary analysis shows that no medical problem has been addressed. I am terminating communication now based on security program S-seven six one three on the authority of the chief of security."

"No," the captain ordered, but the computer had already cut communication.

"This is very odd," The Doctor said.

"It's a lot worse than odd," said Janeway as she touched her forehead briefly before heading out the door. She had had enough of being confined. Her head hurt, that was all. The Doctor had his tests. And she had a ship to run.

She returned to the bridge but didn't take her

seat. Instead she asked Mr. Tuvok into her private office. "Mr. Tuvok," she began as soon as the door had closed. "It seems that we have a security problem. And Ensign Mandel has been confined to her quarters, unable to communicate except in medical emergency, and she tells me that she has the answer to the computer problems that are keeping us here."

The Vulcan nodded. "I am still concerned about the possibility of sabotage. I do not feel it is advisable at this time to give Ensign Mandel direct access to the operating system."

"Whether it is advisable or not, Mr. Tuvok, it is against regulations to confine a crew member to quarters without my knowledge." Janeway massaged her temples. At this point she couldn't decide if her headache stemmed from her injuries or from pure tension.

"Yes, Captain," the security officer replied. "However, due to the extraordinary nature of the circumstances, logic dictated . . ."

"We'll discuss this at greater length after the crisis is over, Mr. Tuvok," Janeway said crisply. The Doctor may have declared her fit to command a starship, but she knew her limits. It would be several days before she would be up to arguing logic with a Vulcan.

Janeway sighed and looked at the console that sat innocently on her worktable. She brushed it with her fingertips as she thought, as if somehow the computer were one of Chakotay's talismans and would guide her. No such luck.

"Who besides Ensign Mandel and Harry is capable of looking at her work and then pulling it apart to make sure there is no sabotage involved?" the captain asked herself, musing. There had to be someone. Or something. Or some way around it.

"I am afraid that Mandel and Kim are our best programmers," Tuvok replied.

"Which means that unless someone is as good as she is, she could slip something by," the captain said thoughtfully. "If she's a saboteur. But if she's right, then we've got to act. And the sooner the better." She paused for a moment and thought. Her head pounded and she pressed her hand against her forehead again. Not that it made any difference, but it helped define the pain as opposed to the problem.

She had looked over the updated supply reports while she had been in sickbay. The Doctor couldn't refuse her that, and even if he had, Neelix had come in to visit Kes while she was on duty. It was easy enough to engage Neelix in conversation. Indeed, the trick was getting him to stop. Especially when the topic involved his beloved kitchen.

"I hate to tell you, Captain, but we're running very low on those Tasalian cabbages. The ones everyone likes so much. Especially when I stuff it with grated onion and Chorean steak. We've completely run out of steak, but I do have another recipe for the cabbage. This one with those apples and tubers, the way I made it a few months ago? Only now we're running out of cabbage. After that last stop, I thought we had enough to last for a year at least. Well, that's what happens when something's popular."

Neelix had only paused to take a breath, but Janeway jumped in. "What about other foodstuffs?" she interjected.

Neelix shook his head, his mouth pressed in a tense line. "As the morale officer, I have to say that rationing is a very bad move. People worry. It makes them insecure. But as your chef, I have to say that I will have to get very—inventive in order for there to be enough. And we'll have to follow a very healthful diet. Maybe The Doctor and Kes can help. We know that a vegetarian diet is low in fat, and far too many cultures have overpraised protein. In fact, most sentient creatures need far less protein than they consider normal. We'll have to make a real campaign of it, but I think it can be done.

"However, my cookies have been very popular. I've set out trays of them near the replicators, so when people have wanted a quick snack, they could find something wholesome immediately without draining any power."

Captain Janeway couldn't repress a slight smile. She appreciated his irrepressible imagination.

"How long do we have before you have to get too

creative? Or we have to get much too healthy?" the captain pursued the question.

"Oh, ten or twelve days," Neelix said. "I can probably squeeze out two more with stew."

"Stew. Yes," Janeway said managing to catch herself before she winced too obviously. Neelix's stews were not among her favorite meals. Though to be honest, it was better than his coffee substitute.

Her mind started to wander, and she brought herself briskly under control. The tendency to drift off from the topics at hand was part of the trauma, she knew, but it was one symptom she could keep firmly in hand, as long as she was aware it was happening.

"Neelix, I think you're tiring the captain," Kes said. "She is supposed to be resting, not making conversation about next week's menu."

Kes gave the captain a pointed look, and so Janeway let the medical assistant lead the Talaxian away. She had gotten the information she needed, at least. Supplies were running out faster than they had anticipated while the ship was still stalled here.

It was as if it was planned. As if the loss of foodstuffs was directly proportional to the time they spent trapped by their own computer.

"The tachyon field," the captain muttered. "I wonder . . . Doctor, could you come here for a moment? I have a theory . . ."

The Doctor appeared with a disapproving look.

"You are here to rest, Captain, and to recover. All this excitement isn't going to help you."

"Doctor, is it possible that the bombardment of the tachyon field is breaking down the cell structure of our fresh food, causing it to spoil?" Janeway asked urgently.

"It could be," The Doctor said hesitantly. "I don't believe that any work has been done in the area. Certainly, none that I'm aware of. But everything in the environment is constantly bombarded with tachyons. Most living creatures have evolved a degree of protection. And the particles are so small as to be undetectable from a life-sign point of view."

"Well, something is ruining our food supply," Janeway said. "Could you look into it? Kes can have Neelix bring up samples of the ruined vegetables."

"That isn't precisely my specialty," The Doctor protested.

Janeway just looked at him. "This is the closest thing we have to a bio lab on board, and you are the closest we have to a biologist," the captain reminded him. "Besides, you'll be losing at least one patient very soon, since I'm leaving as soon as you certify me fit, which had better be in the next half hour."

"Captain, I can't guarantee that."

"Doctor, you had better. Or I'll walk out of sickbay without your authorization."

The Doctor looked at her and blinked. "Yes, I see your point. Kes, bring over that medical tricorder. No, the one on my desk that's already set for the captain's scan."

The Doctor and Kes were so involved they didn't see Janeway's small smile.

CHAPTER
15

THE CAPTAIN WAS ON THE BRIDGE AND TALKING TO
Tuvok. She knew enough about the situation to
know it was critical. Which was to say, she knew
more than anyone else.

"Why do you think Mandel can't be trusted?"
she asked again.

The Vulcan looked at her quizzically. "She refused any offer of help, would not permit anyone
else to work with her or go over her analysis, was
secretive and would not divulge her methodology.
Certainly that is enough, given current conditions,
to warrant inspection."

Janeway hesitated. Her head was splitting, and
the conflict was just beginning. "Tuvok, you know
that I have the greatest respect for your abilities,"

she began carefully, framing her ideas as she spoke. "We've worked together a long time, and you know more than anyone about ship's security." Then she sighed deeply. "But unless Harry is fit for duty in the next few hours, we're going to need Ensign Mandel, no matter how suspicious her behavior. Because, very simply, no one else can do the job. And if we don't get out of here soon, we are going to starve. It's that simple. Something is spoiling our fresh food supply. I've gotten a very disturbing report from Neelix about the high rate of spoilage. If this keeps up, we're not going to be able to make the next supply stop."

Vulcans insist they have no emotions, and they never show them. Still, what could be seen on Tuvok's face might be classified at least as concern. But then, concern is not an emotion. It was also the only logical reaction to the news that they were facing not only possible sabotage and computer failure but starvation as well.

"Captain, do you have any information on the cause of the destroyed foodstuffs?" Tuvok asked.

Janeway shook her head. "The Doctor is looking into it. I suspect that this tachyon bombardment might be part of the problem, but I'm not a biologist."

"And neither is Ensign Mandel," Tuvok said thoughtfully. He paused for a moment, his eyes not focused on the ready room but somewhere beyond in his own calculations. "Captain, it is highly unlikely that the food shortage and the computer problems are unrelated. Given this new data, I would suggest that Ensign Mandel is not responsible. Not unless she has a lot more training and background than we suspect. Which, if she is a Cardassian agent, she would have."

"Which is the problem," Janeway acknowledged heavily. "But we have to assess the alternative risks. If we don't let Mandel work on the program, we're out of food and we can't move. If we let her work on the problem and she's not an agent, we have some possibility of getting out of here."

"And if we let her work on the problem and she is a Cardassian agent . . ."

"We're no worse off than we are if we don't give her access," the captain said firmly. "And if she is a Cardassian agent, there is still no reason to think that she has orders to destroy *Voyager* and herself with it. As I recall, the Obsidian Order doesn't like to lose operatives after they've invested so much in training and surgery.

"No, Mr. Tuvok, we have a lot more to worry about than a Cardassian spy. Or any kind of spy. Though if she is one, we will have to deal with that later. After we get out of here."

"Very well, Captain. I shall release her."

Janeway nodded. "And let her know about the other problems, the food shortage and the fact that we're not close to the next supply stop, which she should be aware of anyway. Stellar Cartography is one area where they actually are aware of these things, but she won't know that we're critical on supplies. Tell her."

If a Vulcan could look perturbed, Mr. Tuvok did. "I must point out to you that I am skeptical of this course of action," the Vulcan said. "I would be remiss in my duty were I not to inform you of that."

"Yes, I understand that, Mr. Tuvok." Then Janeway sighed. "The problem is somewhere in the command system. It's not the hardware. If it were, then Torres could fix it. If it were anything else, we would have located it by now. The real problem is that we are so dependent on our computer and on its initial operating system that we aren't even aware of how many of its problems can carry over into everything else. The dependency is more dangerous than any agent."

"It does make us vulnerable," Tuvok agreed.

"If we could only compartmentalize it the way we do life-support," the captain said. And then she thought for a moment. "Once we get past this, I might ask Ensign Mandel to work on a design to do that. With Mr. Kim. It might keep the two of them occupied in their free time."

Tuvok appeared nonplussed. "I will fetch Ensign Mandel and explain our supply situation."

Janeway thanked him and let him go. She knew it was his job to be concerned about the security of the ship. She was certainly concerned about security as well. But what would be a reasonable course of action in the Alpha Quadrant where they could get to a Star Base, where ships of the Federation were all around, and where their technology was readily available simply wasn't an option out here.

No, Tuvok understood that, Janeway told herself. He understood it as well as she did, as well as they all did. Only that didn't mean that they had to like it. And she had said that she was running a Federation ship. She meant it, too, right down to the last line. But sometimes there weren't alternatives out here. Sometimes all she could do was choose the lesser of two evils.

Her head began throbbing violently again. This wasn't the injury. This was command. This was having to take them home when the odds were so heavily stacked against them.

It was like being trapped in a desert, in a sinkhole. In quicksand.

Quicksand. Something that appeared solid but was a trap underneath. That sat passive until something came along.

They had fallen into such a trap. Captain Janeway knew it. This was nothing to do with Cardassians or spies or anything they had left behind in the Alpha Quadrant. This was something that was directly related to the dead alien ships in the center of the tachyon field.

Why were all these ships dead, and some of them still transmitting? Why was there a tachyon field? And why had she and many of *Voyager's* crew felt so lonely?

Suddenly, the questions reversed and the logic fell into place. What if the dead ships were lonely, looking for company? That would make sense. Then they would send out some kind of communication, drawing in like-minded beings.

So far so good. Only, how could dead ships be lonely? There were no life-signs there. Nothing at all had been alive. She had been there and she knew.

Her head throbbed and threatened to explode. She could see the answer. She knew she knew, if only she could quiet the pain. If only . . .

No, she suddenly realized that she was losing focus again. She wanted to be angry with the state of medicine. They should be able to give her something so that she could just do her job without fear that her mind would wander. Though injury to the brain was hardly a minor problem.

Still, she wished the Doctor had something in his bag of tricks to get rid of the headache and keep her from distractions. And while she was certain that she had chosen the best course of action in the matter of Daphne Mandel and the operating system, she still was uneasy. She had worked with Tuvok for many years and trusted him implicitly. He had instincts, though he would disapprove of that description of his ability, and when he distrusted someone she knew it was for good reason.

If only Harry Kim were back on duty. No, she realized, she should be glad that he was still alive.

But thinking about Kim brought her back to what she had discovered when they had investigated the alien craft.

She remembered the computer log they had downloaded. That shouldn't take a wild talent to analyze. And there should be plenty hidden in that document, no matter how little they had gotten out of the log before they were injured.

The captain touched her commbadge. "Engineering, have you recovered the tricorder that Mr. Kim had on the away mission?"

"No, Captain. What tricorder?" B'Elanna Torres was trying very hard not to sound harassed, Janeway could tell. Torres couldn't disguise an emotion if her life depended on it.

"I'll have someone bring it down," Janeway said. "We downloaded the logs of the alien ship, and I think something in that might tell us what's wrong. It looks like they suffered the same problems we're having."

"I'll get on it as soon as I have it," Torres promised. "And I'll go up and get it. Have to look in on Harry, anyway. Try to remind him he's got work to do, he can't lie in bed sleeping while the rest of us are on emergency rating. Maybe I'll bring him some cookies."

Janeway chuckled. She'd been eating the cookies herself, and they were definitely the best thing Neelix had made in a very long time. Then she called sickbay and made certain they could locate the tricorder. As she had suspected, it had been sitting in a pile with the rest of Kim's clothing and equipment, completely forgotten. Even though the situation was critical, she felt a surge of assurance. Now she had the key, she had remembered the critical detail.

Now she could return to the bridge and face her crew.

"You know, Harry, you're one lazy, green sluga-bed," B'Elanna Torres said. "Here we are stuck with the computer down, bugs in the operating system, a drive that won't listen to us, and you're lazing around in bed."

"Uuuugghh," Harry Kim replied.

Kes smiled brightly. "That's the most communicative he's been," she whispered to the chief engineer.

"Well, that's not good enough," Torres replied, not looking away from Kim's bandaged face. "I need help, Harry Kim. You're the best programmer on this ship, and we're going to have to run this alien analysis without you until you make up your mind to get out of bed and do your job."

"Nnnn mmmm jb," Kim tried to say. His eyes were on her, alert and aware.

"What do you mean it's not your job?" Torres was honestly angry now. "Maybe it isn't on your duty roster, but believe me, the captain will reas-sign you if necessary to make this work. You're the only one who can do it, besides that Daphne Mandel person. And she's too out in the theory ozone to do anything practical. Meaningful."

"Srrreee." Kim tried to apologize.

B'Elanna Torres snorted. "If you were Klingon, you'd get up right now," she berated him. "Since you're not, we're going to have to try to do this without you, which, believe me, isn't going to be easy. You owe me for this one, Kim."

"Dsssrrrr," Harry mumbled.

"You're in luck," Torres came back quickly, understanding only too well. "Neelix finally made something decent. You'd think these cookies came out of that little bakery near Starfleet Headquarters."

Kim blinked, tried to smile, but couldn't move that much. He made a sound that Torres took for assent.

"Lieutenant Torres, much as we appreciate your assistance in bringing Mr. Kim to consciousness, you are now tiring the patient. You must leave now. You can come back tomorrow." The Doctor ordered B'Elanna out with no sympathy whatever.

Which the engineer appreciated. She liked the fact that The Doctor was so protective of Harry. She was still angry at her friend for letting himself get this badly hurt, and she was terribly worried for him. Not that she'd admit it, of course.

She liked Harry Kim. Of course, there was no one on *Voyager* who didn't like him. But she also respected his abilities and had come to depend on his assistance even though, technically, working in Engineering wasn't part of his job.

He had volunteered to help out so many times that she had come to view him with a somewhat proprietary attitude. After all, she really needed him. And he liked working in Engineering. He did special projects in his free time, as if it were his hobby.

Secretly, B'Elanna had hopes of turning him into a real engineer. He had the feel for it, more than Lt. Carey. Who, she finally had to admit, was a good colleague and an excellent manager. And an adequate if somewhat pedestrian engineer.

But Harry, Harry had the imagination and the intuition. He could *feel* the way things should work. And he had the math to back it up.

But no matter how much she needed him right now, The Doctor wasn't going to let him go early on her account.

"He is much better," Kes said softly at her shoulder.

B'Elanna turned sharply. She hadn't been aware of Kes's presence as the young medical assistant accompanied her into the corridor. "What?" Torres asked briskly.

Kes handed over the tricorder. "I think you forgot this," she said, and smiled. "Really, it's good that you came up. I think that you brought Harry back a little closer to us. And if he knows that there are good problems to work on when he's ready, he'll want to be ready. And he won't be as bored. Being a patient can be very boring."

"Why are you telling me this?" Torres demanded. She found Kes's soft manner confusing.

"Because I want you to know that while Harry is in no condition to do anything productive, as he improves, he might be able to think about your problems and follow the adjustments. It would certainly take his mind off his troubles. And even if he can't actually contribute, in a day or two he'll be able to at least scan something for errors."

That last sentiment made sense to Torres. In fact, if she was hearing correctly, the assistant was saying that Harry would be ready to work on the project by tomorrow. Only they would have to call it something else, and he would have to stay in sickbay.

That was good enough for B'Elanna.

B'Elanna wished the Ocampa would just say things directly rather than hint and indicate. But Kes was one of those healer types who saw physical health and well-being as the most important possible goal in life.

B'Elanna Torres found that attitude incomprehensible. It was obvious to her that the first duty of anyone aboard a spacecraft was to make certain that the ship ran. That the engines were powered, that the warp core was intact, that there was power for all of *Voyager*'s major systems. She could not imagine any other task being so absorbing, so fascinating, or nearly so important.

As she returned to Engineering, she wondered why she found this particular situation so frustrating. She had been in worse circumstances. She had even enjoyed the challenge of emergency repairs, or needing to make sudden changes in configuration to accommodate new conditions.

But this time she hated what was happening. She couldn't solve it, she couldn't even talk to her systems. And that was the real problem. The computer was not her true area of expertise. She had to rely on someone else to do the job, and she was never happy about that.

Moreover, she had to rely on Daphne Mandel.

Mandel was smart, certainly, maybe even brilliant. But she was also selfish and self-indulgent.

And now Mandel had disappeared because she was too much of a prima donna to work decently with Tuvok. Torres wanted to scream. It was hard to need the services of someone she never wanted to see again.

She couldn't do this one alone. She couldn't go that deeply into the operating system. She didn't have the talent for that as she did for more mechanical things. It was all so much mumbo jumbo to her.

So she was shocked and more than a little ambivalent when she arrived in Engineering to find Daphne Mandel back at the direct contact workstation. Tuvok stood next to the cartographer, so B'Elanna did not immediately order her from the premises. Instead, she pulled the Vulcan aside.

"What is she doing here?" Torres hissed.

"Captain's orders," Tuvok said. "Supplies are critical. If we do not leave here very soon, we will run out of food before we get to the next supply stop."

B'Elanna wanted to break something. Preferably someone's bones, but if they weren't available, the computer would do. It was at the center of this mess, after all she had done.

"Have you scanned the alien log yet?" Tuvok asked.

B'Elanna blinked. She had the tricorder in her hand and had forgotten it completely.

"I don't know how this will work given the computer malfunction," she admitted.

"Oh, the problem only relates to the drive and engines, and navigation and the helm," Mandel called out from her terminal. "It shouldn't affect analytic abilities at all."

"How reassuring," Torres said, and then inserted the tricorder into a download slot and told the computer to analyze.

At first the screen display filled with a mishmash of alien symbols in bright green on an orange background. Eyes glued to the screen hoping to make some kind of sense of it all, B'Elanna knew it was hopeless. Without a lot more help from the translation center of the computer they were lost.

Besides, the neon colors flashed to red on turquoise and then electric blue on pink. Just looking at the screen hurt her eyes.

The picture changed to what appeared to be the interior of the alien ship, with a single creature at the center. The lights on the projections in this sequence were not a crazy jumble at all but glowed a steady pale pink that gave the alien speaker's face a warm cast. A very few indicators showed amber or green, and B'Elanna realized that the colors were real codes and that the mess the away team had seen was the aftermath of destruction when everything had gone wild.

The alien was like none she had ever seen. There was nothing to scale, but she recognized that the four arms were resting on projections that were about the height of her shoulders. Its skin was a soft, warmish gray, though B'Elanna thought the color could be a result of the lights. And its face, while utterly inhuman, showed sorrow and intelligence and a kind of confused resignation that seemed all too human.

It appeared as if the alien's mouth was moving, but no sound came out. There was a lag.

"Band search," Torres ordered the computer.

Then the voice came through the speaker. It was not the computer's usual bland female voice, but one deeper and gravelly. Male, and tense, Torres thought immediately. Words rushed out, each of them falling over the others, all of them completely meaningless at first in their original language.

And then it changed. The voice remained, but the words became comprehensible. The translation center was working. If the translation was accurate.

"We are being consumed by this creature, which is no living thing but the evil spawn of consciousness," the alien voice said. "The deterioration has increased geometrically. The longer we are here, the faster our food spoils, the faster our power is drained. We are not sure which we will lose first—life-support or food.

"In any case, we are beyond help. We have called on the gods to no avail, and we have called on our elders to give us guidance in this extremity. But our elders have been silent, and the gods are content to laugh at our suffering. So be it. To amuse the gods is no small thing.

"If they are our gods. There are some here who say our enemy wears the guises of the Beloveds only in order to entrap us. But how could this alien thing, this construct, know who it is we worship? Or who we think is the Created of Beauty?

"And so we are frozen here, watching ourselves die. Nothing is worse than this waiting, knowing that there is no hope, that forever is declared."

There was a long static burst on the screen as the picture broke up.

"Is there any more?" Tuvok asked. "Computer, advance to next entry."

B'Elanna Torres blinked away a stray tear as she looked at the Vulcan. As she noticed the other members of her team at their stations, she realized that only Tuvok showed no reaction. Even Daphne Mandel was watching, no longer lost in her own universe of code. Mandel's eyes were wide and soft with a compassion that Torres thought she reserved only for machines.

"There are no more entries," the computer said in its usual voice.

"Computer, go back as far as possible and begin translation in text format," Torres said. She didn't want to hear the story of the destruction of this ship in the pained, ragged voice of the dying captain. Text would cover all the important information without upsetting her entire department even more. There was certainly enough work to be done that they couldn't afford to listen—and think of how closely their own situation paralleled that of this alien.

And yet, the knowledge of what had happened to the aliens was hauntingly familiar. They had fallen into a trap, a thing that somehow knew more about them than it ought and was able to entice them until it drained all their resources and they died.

Voyager was not going to suffer that fate, Torres decided. Not if B'Elanna Torres had anything at all to do with it. To live, to fight, to go on and go home.

And yet at her core she knew that part of her will to fight was for that alien captain who had cared so deeply for his ship, for his people. She would make sure that his words reached their home.

CHAPTER
16

HARRY KIM HURT. HIS HEAD HURT, HIS BACK HURT, and his right side hurt most of all. But he wasn't nearly as hurt as he was bored in sickbay. At least The Doctor had finally let him sit up. And Kes had brought over a monitor for him to watch Daphne Mandel's debugging procedure.

She was good, he had to give her that. She was more than good. And that made him feel even more useless.

It didn't help that when Kes arrived with lunch, his tray contained soup and crackers and a very bland baked tuber that Neelix usually fixed with spices and vegetables. But for sickbay it was dead plain and dull, and if he hadn't been so hungry, he would have ignored it altogether. How did they expect someone to get well on such boring food?

"It's motivation," Kes told him when she came to clear the tray away. "You know that in order to get anything you like, you have to get well."

"Fine. I want to get well anyway. I am well, really. Just a couple of aches that'll go away with a little time and exercise. And a decent diet."

Kes picked up the tray. "You're supposed to rest now," she told Kim. "If The Doctor comes back and finds you working . . ."

"I'm not working," Kim grumbled. "I wish I were working. At least then I'd have something to think about other than every time my side twinges. And I'd get some of that onion hot sauce for this thing. Do you think maybe you could get me some hot sauce for dinner?"

Kes considered for a moment. "If you will go back to bed now and sleep for a few hours, I will try to get you hot sauce. Or at least some kind of sauce."

Harry Kim thought about the benefits of the trade, and with a sigh, he got up and returned to his medical bed with all the attachments and readouts. To be honest, he was tired. Sitting up like that had been hard, and it was the first day he was really able to leave the bed at all.

Still, he had too much pride to let on quite how exhausting even simple things were. And he was honestly bored out of his mind.

He lay there, half drifting but not quite asleep, when someone hissed by his bedside. "Harry, hey

Harry, c'mon. If you don't wake up, they'll catch me and I'll get thrown out again."

In a slightly slurred voice Harry asked, "Again?" He didn't remember any visitors. He had a strange dream with B'Elanna on the alien ship, and a few times Tom Paris and Tuvok and Captain Janeway had drifted through his semiconscious fantasies. Now for the first time he questioned whether those were entirely illusion or if maybe some of it really had happened.

"I brought you something," the voice whispered again.

Harry opened his eyes slowly. It took him a moment to focus and recognize Tom Paris. Tom was holding out something wrapped in foil.

"Take it, take it fast before The Doctor catches us," Paris hissed. "It's Maderlion hot dumplings with Tla gravy and a double Vulcan mocha, extra sweet."

Harry's eyes were suddenly clear and he felt wide awake. "Vulcan mocha? Maderlion hot dumplings?" he asked, hoping that this was no dream, that he wouldn't wake up and find out that Kes hadn't even gotten his hot sauce. Maderlion hot dumplings were something he hadn't tasted in months, not since he had decided to use his replicator rations for more useful objects. Or at least less ration-intensive foodstuffs. "How did you get them?" he asked.

Paris just smiled. "I figured you could use something to cheer you up and get you mending so that you can help clean out this computer mess. Because, Harry, you and this drip Daphne Mandel are the only people on *Voyager* who know enough about debugging operating systems to be trusted with this job."

"Made a real ugly mess," Harry agreed. "But Mandel is doing okay. I've been watching when they let me."

"Yeah, well, okay isn't good enough. And it isn't fast enough, either. The captain has called a staff meeting a couple of hours from now to discuss that log you got on the tricorder before the explosion, do you remember?"

"Of course I remember."

"Well, I thought you might be interested to know what it says. While you eat your dumplings, of course."

"But . . ." Harry protested.

"You can't hide them," Paris insisted. "They'll just take them away. And that would be a real waste, since I just used two days of replicator rations to get them for you."

Kim didn't waste a moment opening the package and picking up one of the warm dumplings covered in thick sauce. He hesitated for a moment, realizing that there were no utensils available. He really didn't want to eat with his fingers, but there was no choice. And he was so hungry.

"So we've got the condensed text version. Basically, what it says is that this alien ship we were on had all the same problems we have. Only they also had a progressive problem with food spoilage as well. They couldn't connect to their drive, and their computer refused all data from the helm and navigation. They got their best computer people on it, and they thought it looked like a virus, but they couldn't understand how something so specific to their operating system could be written by someone who wasn't one of their own high-level computer people.

"So they started a purge. They were looking for a saboteur. And all the time they had these messages and 'visions' of what they thought were their gods. Or images of their gods."

"Just like us seeing the angels," Harry said between bites. He had only one dumpling left, and he wanted to make it last. He had forgotten just how delicious they were, the perfect balance of spicy hot and vinegar sharp. He licked his fingers where the juice had run over them.

"Exactly. Only how could our angels be their gods?"

"Maybe because they're the same beings," Kim suggested. "Maybe these same beings have traveled all over the entire galaxy. Maybe they are related to the Caretaker and can travel even farther."

"Exactly. The Caretaker's race," Paris said, his eyes gleaming. "And if we can find them, or the one of them that is creating this whole thing, we could get home."

"If," Kim reminded him. "I don't want to get too hopeful. I would hate to be disappointed. You didn't happen to bring any dessert, did you?"

Captain Janeway had gathered her staff officers in her ready room to view the entirety of the log they had brought back from the alien ship. Chakotay was glad that he was there, that he was awake, and that he had just slept for five hours. He would have preferred longer, but even his restless, dream-filled sleep had restored some of his natural balance.

Besides, though he could not remember the dream clearly, he knew that his animal guide had visited him again. Even here, so far from the ancestral lands, it was with him. The dream made him wake reassured, confident. And he vaguely suspected that he had been told exactly what needed to be done, only he couldn't remember. Not now. When he needed the knowledge it would be there, planted in his mind. Part of the "instinct," he was certain. Just that most people didn't even have the shreds of memory about the dreams their power animals gave them. And he had an inspiration that he was certain came from that dream, one that he knew was important.

"I think Kes should be here, too," Chakotay said. "She came with me to rescue you, and she seemed to know that there would be some danger. If there is some kind of empathic communication going on,

Kes is in the loop. And I think that her input could be valuable."

The captain nodded. "If she has had some sort of telepathic communication with these people, she might be able to recognize them. Or their holograms. I don't know enough about those talents to rule anything out. Call her in and we'll get started."

Chakotay did call her in, and then the captain asked, "Could you fill us in on why you believe she has this telepathic contact?"

Chakotay looked away from both the captain and Tuvok. He leaned forward and carefully recounted the story of his decision to launch an ad hoc rescue mission before the away team was due to check in. Then he sat back and braced himself for Janeway's and Tuvok's reactions.

There was a hush in the ready room. Finally the captain broke the silence. "You took the shuttle-craft over to the alien ship *before* the explosion?"

Chakotay looked at her steadily. "Yes. I did. I can't explain it now, only then I was certain that you were in trouble. Though there was no reason to think that at the time. So I got there just in time for the explosion."

The captain and Tom Paris studied him. Then the captain said very gently, "Have you thought that perhaps Kes is not the only one who might have had some kind of empathic contact?"

Chakotay breathed deeply. "I have wondered about that. But then, I have also been trained to be aware of my own hunches and to follow them. I haven't felt anything that seemed—invasive."

He had searched for the word. Thinking about those moments when he had been so lonely he thought he would die, he knew that the feeling had not come from within. "Although as we entered the tachyon field I did notice a certain feeling of loneliness that I don't think came from me," he said softly. "I was pretty unhappy for a while, but that was all. It isn't important."

"No, Commander, it may be very important," the captain said. "Loneliness. That makes some kind of sense. But the rest still doesn't."

"I felt that, too, Captain," Kes said. They had all been so intent on Chakotay's experience that they had not noticed her arrival.

"I had very disturbing dreams, all of them about loneliness, all in situations where I hadn't remembered feeling so much lonely as angry or afraid," Kes continued. "But the dreams felt very much as if they were mine, only the emotions were changed."

"Kes, why did you meet me at the shuttlebay? How did you know I was going after the away team?" Chakotay asked.

"I didn't know," Kes said. "I just had a very strong need to try to go after them myself. I was certain that something had gone wrong, and The Doctor can't go, so I was the only alternative."

"You know, it seems like both of you are sensitive to whatever telepathic projection this thing has," Tom Paris spoke up. "I wonder if it just projected something and then you both were compelled by the same thought to come after us. As if it was planning to create the explosion and wanted to evacuate us, or at least get us out of there."

"That is the most logical explanation," Tuvok agreed.

"But what is it trying to communicate?" Kes asked.

"That's pretty self-evident," Tom Paris said with disgust. "It is lonely. It wants us to stay. It's like some spider thats trapped us in its web and now it wants us to feel sorry for it and be good buddies. Until we die, like the other ship."

"I don't think so," Kes said softly. "It doesn't feel that way at all to me. I don't think that whatever I've been feeling means harm."

"Yeah, well, the spider probably doesn't mean harm either," Paris retorted. "It probably is just sitting there thinking about dinner. It has no desire to hurt anyone. Just to eat."

"Why don't we find out what's in the log?" B'Elanna interrupted. "I don't know about you, but I've got work to get back to."

"I don't want to display the entire thing," Janeway said.

"By now you should have been able to read the text version with the technically salient points. I want each of you to look at that data in terms of your own departments. Together with this new information, maybe we can piece out what's going on. And how to stop it."

Tuvok spoke first. "Captain, it appears that these aliens fell into precisely the same trap we did, which would logically rule out any Cardassian interference or sabotage. There is evidence in this log of similar food spoilage problems, computer breakdown, and the disconnect from navigation that we have experienced. And while it is not unreasonable to suspect sabotage, given the circumstances, with this document it seems highly unlikely. I do not see any way in which a Cardassian agent could have planted this log."

"Or tampered with it?" Janeway asked.

Tuvok took a moment and looked thoughtful. "I think not, Captain. No one except the away team knew anything about the log until Lt. Torres took it from sickbay. It was in her possession the whole time until she had the computer do the translation. And we have the traces on the translation. There was no outside interference. The computer alone had access to the documents."

"But what about after, when the text was compiled and sent to us?" Chakotay asked. "Documents could be changed then and we wouldn't know."

Tuvok nodded gravely. "That is true, Commander. And because both Lt. Torres and I were aware that that was the weak link in the cycle, we took two precautions. First, we embedded a second code string in the document. If there were any tampering, it would show up in a very simple diagnostic that revealed the embedded sequence. So if everyone has access to their files open now, we can have the computer extract the sequence. B'Elanna?"

B'Elanna gave the computer a few quick instructions, and then Tom Paris began laughing.

"I do not see what is so funny, Mr. Paris," Tuvok said.

"It says, 'If you can read this message there is no spy tampering,'" B'Elanna Torres said simply. "I don't see why that's so hilarious. It's very straightforward. I wrote it myself."

Tom Paris rolled his eyes. Chakotay smiled and shook his head. The captain smiled just a little and waited until everyone had regained their composure before leading the meeting to the next point. "So we know that we don't have a Cardassian saboteur aboard."

"Not precisely, Captain," Tuvok corrected her. "We know that this situation is not the result of sabotage. That does not mean that we do not have a spy aboard."

"Agreed, Mr. Tuvok," the captain said.

The captain continued. "The log discusses the same kind of computer breakdown we've experienced. And they were unable to fix the problem and take control of their engines. So, in essence, they were trapped."

"Correct, Captain," B'Elanna Torres agreed. "But I haven't seen their computer configuration, so I don't know how their systems interacted and how interdependent they were. With our own system, as soon as Ensign Mandel gets all the garbage code out of the operating system, we should have immediate access to the helm again."

"And what if the alien transmits another set of instructions?" Tuvok asked.

"Now that we know how it embeds code, we can protect against it. Essentially, think of this as a computer virus. Once we have the idea of how the virus works, it isn't hard to protect ourselves. It's just knowing what to protect against."

Tuvok's eyebrows went up. "Indeed. I wish I had access to similar security."

B'Elanna blinked. "But you do. You've got the best virus protection that Starfleet wrote. And believe me, I know. You don't know how many viruses I tried to write to worm into that system."

"Indeed?"

"Let's forget about this," Chakotay interrupted. "Tuvok, you know who and what we were. None of us are going to be ashamed of being Maquis."

B'Elanna Torres shrugged. "I am ashamed that I'm not a good enough programmer to have cracked any of the Starfleet protections anyway. Though Daphne Mandel or Harry Kim might be able to, if you gave them enough time and didn't change any of the parameters."

"This is not helping us figure out the current problem," the captain chided them. "Let's stick to the topic. We know that this alien vessel suffered from the same sequence of symptoms that are affecting *Voyager*. We know that they tried to take manual control of engines and failed. We know that they were somehow enticed by images of beings that appeared to be their gods or 'beautiful ones.'"

"Like those angelic beings we saw." Tom Paris said. "Whatever is creating the problem somehow adapts the creatures to whoever is looking."

"And if this thing can take over a computer system, it would have no trouble reconfiguring the holodeck programs to project those beings," Chakotay added.

"So we're basically dealing with a life-form that takes over computer systems and reads code into their operating systems. With or without a universal translator. It doesn't appear that the aliens had one," the captain summed up. "But we don't know where whatever it is that's doing this is located. We have no life-form readings at all from any of these dead ships."

"If we can trust our readings," Tuvok added. "Our computer security has been invaded. We don't know what areas have been compromised. We must assume one being exists somewhere in this nexus and is evading detection."

"So we have to find and identify whoever it is," Kes said quietly.

"No," Torres replied. "All we have to do is fix our own connections and get out of here."

"And leave it to hunt down and trap someone else?" The medical assistant pursued her line of reasoning.

"We can't get rid of every bad guy in the galaxy," Paris said. "But I wouldn't mind trying with this one. It's already collected quite a little graveyard around here. And I think starving people to death is the lowest form . . ."

"What if it isn't some bad guy at all?" Kes asked. "What if it just has a different point of view? Maybe it thinks it is doing something beneficial."

"Cleaning every living species out of the area?" Paris retorted. "Sorry, by my definition, that's a bad guy."

"Wait a second, Paris, Kes has a point," Chakotay interrupted. "We thought of the Caretaker as harming us, while it was trying to fulfill what it perceived as its obligation to the Ocampa. And if this is in any way related to the Caretaker's companion, then it would be a very good idea to locate it."

The captain let the thought settle before she spoke. "I have been considering that possibility," she announced. "If this is the Caretaker's companion, then we might just have found the way home. And even if it is not the companion, there are technologies here that are different from ours.

Whatever is operating here is extremely sophisticated and might have the capability of helping us get back. Even if it's only half the way, that's a big jump."

"What about the shortages?" Chakotay asked.

The captain sighed. "We're going to have to work quickly. I will not pass up the opportunity to access a technology that might get us home. But I also refuse to endanger the lives of this crew through shortages. Which means that I am sending another away team." The captain rose. "Chakotay, Paris, and B'Elanna, I want the three of you to be ready to leave within the hour. Your mission has two goals. Your first goal is to gather as much information as you can on the being that has trapped us, and how the trap is set. The second is to search for relevant transportation technology."

"Captain, can we take Ensign Mandel along for computer analysis?" B'Elanna requested. "Both goals would be served a lot faster with someone of her caliber of computer expertise around."

The captain frowned. "She has quite a job cleaning out that program infestation."

"Captain, Harry Kim is still not well enough to leave sickbay, but he is alert and he's getting very bored. In fact, I don't know if The Doctor can keep him under observation much longer. But if you were to assign him that task, he could interface through the sickbay priority terminal, and we could keep him where we can take care of him if he has any trouble."

Captain Janeway smiled. "So Harry's well enough to be a bad patient? That's good news. Then, yes, by all means take Ensign Mandel. Dismissed."

CHAPTER
17

"I CAN'T LEAVE NOW," ENSIGN MANDEL INFORMED Chakotay. "I'm in the middle of getting rid of the junk that's keeping us here. Which is much more important than whatever away mission you've got in mind."

Daphne Mandel remained in her seat at the Engineering workstation. She didn't even glance from the lines of code scrolling past at an impossible rate. She just outright ignored him. She was so completely wrapped up in her task that she didn't seem to notice that he hadn't left.

Chakotay was so stunned that he nearly dropped the plate of cookies he'd brought as a peace offering. He had never imagined insubordination on this level. No wonder Tuvok had thought she was a spy. Except a spy would have covered up a bad attitude much better than Ensign Mandel.

Even in the Maquis he had never encountered such poor military bearing and lack of respect. And Chakotay was not about to tolerate it.

"Ensign Mandel, this is Starfleet, and you don't get to say that you're too busy right now. You will accompany the away team to the alien vessel, where your computer skills will be more than well utilized. Ensign Kim can take care of the rest of this task, since you have outlined the parameters so well."

"I thought he was dying," Mandel said glumly.

"He is recovering. Frankly, if he were in better shape, I would prefer to have him along on the mission. Not only is he familiar with the computer we are exploring, he also doesn't have an attitude problem." Chakotay held his voice in check, but he couldn't keep his anger out of what he said. "But he isn't well enough to walk around yet, let alone put on an environmental suit and download alien computer logs in a hostile environment. You are."

At least Chakotay did not say that he would far prefer Harry Kim's company as well. He wanted to, but the discipline of years of leadership had trained him well enough that he was able to bite back the words.

This Ensign Mandel infuriated him. She probably infuriated everybody who knew her. No wonder she was stuck off in Stellar Cartography where she didn't have to deal with human beings.

Chakotay did not have a good feeling about this mission. He was certain the foreboding, or most of it, was strictly his own.

Even if he didn't think much of Mandel's social skills, he had to admit that she, and everyone else on the away team, knew what they were doing. It was a good group. They were going to find the technology needed to get home while *Voyager* broke free of the grip of the program that was embedded in their computer. They were going to . . .

be alone forever. No one would ever understand and they would be trapped in the dark, in the cold. Alone alone alone. Reaching out to life, to warmth, only to be rejected again and again. Why did no one love him? No one ever stayed. . . .

Stop it! Chakotay told himself. It was the alien. These were not his own thoughts.

Still, even as he knew that, he couldn't stop hearing the words in his head.

I do what they say, what they want. I give to them and they all hate me. I need. I need. I can't be alone anymore. Please come to me. Be my friend.

Chakotay sank down in the corridor holding his head in his hands. Resisting it, resisting the thought. Fighting to keep up his own walls, his integrity. He was afraid that the thing would take over his mind . . .

like water. This was another voice. Quieter than the insistent screaming of the alien, and perfectly assured. *Be like water. Now that you know what it is you can let it flow past you and into forever. Let it go.*

He felt the recognition. It was his totem. It had been with him since he had first taken up the quest when he had been taught by his father and medicine chiefs back home. It had always been with him, always given him good advice.

Now it said to flow with it, not to resist.

It was difficult. It was one of the most difficult things Chakotay had ever attempted. To open his mind to what he was certain would be invasion took courage.

Slowly he permitted himself to unclench. To let it be. It was not him, it was not from his being. It was an alien thing, and it was just trying to talk in the way that it knew. He recited that as if it were a mantra. The alien just wants to talk. It does not want your mind. Your mind is your mind. If you let it go, it will flow through you and outward and leave you refreshed and cleaned.

He was not sure if the image was entirely true, but it was enough. He tried to imagine it as separate from himself and greet it as he would any stranger he considered a potential friend.

"Hello, traveler. It is good to meet you in this place."

To me? You talk to me? The alien sounded like a child in his mind. Its emotions certainly were childlike, simple to the extreme.

"Yes, I speak to you," Chakotay answered carefully, as he would a bright and frightened child. "It is going to be fine. Just tell us where we can find you, and you can come with us. You won't be lonely anymore."

The alien child-voice giggled in his mind. *I am here,* it told him. *Here, all of here. Will you stay with me?*

Maybe it was the indigo angel. Maybe it was the hopelessness of the aliens' deaths. Chakotay didn't know, but he did not trust the innocence and fear in the child-voice in his head.

How often had he heard the old adage that telepathic communication couldn't lie? And yet he suspected that what he was hearing was—not exactly a lie, but a misrepresentation.

"We are coming over now," Chakotay said. "We will be there and we will meet you. Will you come out and show yourself? We haven't seen you yet."

Another giggle was muffled quickly. *You have seen me. I am beautiful.*

Chakotay did not reply. He was certain that the angels were malevolent and artificial.

His head hurt from the intrusion, though he knew clearly that it was the only way he could make the thing leave him alone.

You hate me! It screamed at him, anger blasting at him from inside his own skull. *You want to get rid of me. You're just like all the others. All the others. I won't let you.*

"Mr. Chakotay, are you all right?" Kes asked, bending over. She had unslung her medical pack and laid it on the deck, ready to report for the mission.

Chakotay opened his eyes slowly. "I'll be fine. Whatever it is was talking to me. I think I made it angry."

Kes nodded seriously. "I know what you mean. I could feel anger all around when I got off the turbo. At least I'm getting better at knowing when it's it and when it's me."

Chakotay managed a slight smile. "It's just like a spoiled child throwing rocks at grownups," he said wryly. "Which makes it a lot more dangerous than a consciously evil adult."

Kes cocked her head quizzically. "I don't understand," she said. "A child can't do the damage an adult can do."

"Look out there," Chakotay countered. "All those dead ships, all those dead people, because one child is running rampant. Well, come on, let's get to it."

"What are we going to do when we find it?" Kes asked.

"I don't know what anyone else plans to do," Chakotay answered, "but personally, I intend to take it over my knee and give it a good spanking."

"Captain, could I talk to you for a moment?" Harry Kim asked via the comm link. He wanted to get up and go to the bridge himself. He couldn't. The Doctor, or someone, had taken his clothes.

"I'll be down shortly, Mr. Kim," the captain had said.

Harry Kim was a little embarrassed that the captain had to come all the way to sickbay to talk to him. There was the fact that he wasn't really strong enough to make it as far as the turbolift, let alone the bridge. "Maybe tomorrow," Kes had said.

And he certainly was recovering well. Even The Doctor had shown grudging approval. Tom had shown up with a replicated dinner again last night and lunch just two hours ago. He was lucky to have such good friends.

But he could still use another helping of that Andorian spice cake. The last time he had been this hungry was plebe year at the Academy, playing three sports and still growing.

But that still didn't make him feel better about having to ask the captain to come to him instead of going to her with what he had found. And he would at least have preferred to be in uniform, not in the baggy pajamas that The Doctor had insisted that he wear over the various monitors and drug patches affixed to different parts of his body.

"A uniform will only displace them," The Doctor had said preemptively. "And I want those medication distributions in good working order."

Kim knew when he was beaten. So he tried not to think about the clothes, and to tell the truth the pajamas were very comfortable. Though he really would prefer that the captain not see him in such a state of undress.

Being in recovery had not slowed down his mental ability. Sure, he got tired quickly and couldn't sit up for a long period of time. But the frequent breaks where he had nothing to do but lie down and stare at the ceiling had given him the perspective to see exactly what had been done in the operating system.

Daphne Mandel had identified the bogus code, but Kim saw that she hadn't realized everything that the alien had done to them. It was subtle, global, insidious. It was brilliant.

And as he lay with nothing else to occupy him, he began to get an idea of what kind of creature had sabotaged them so effectively. What kind of being could be so very good with their computer language to create what was essentially a virus that wouldn't kill the computer but would eventually destroy *Voyager*.

It was twisted. An enemy would be more straightforward. Kim knew enough about Cardassians, Klingons, and Romulans to know that there was a certain level of honor in enmity. And it frightened Harry Kim in a way other things had not frightened him.

Oh, sure, he'd been scared before. Plenty of times.

But most of his fears were reasonable. This one wasn't. This was something that logic and good sense wouldn't overcome. This was something that was intended to kill them for no reason he could discern.

And the programming was intricate, elegant in a way that inspired his mathematically trained mind. He wanted to create programs like this, make things so utterly efficient and graceful in so very few lines. The perfection of programming was at odds with the functions it delineated. To Harry Kim it was an abomination that a program so perfectly composed should create such utter devastation.

The captain arrived in sickbay. Harry tried to stand, but Janeway waved her hand. "No, Mr. Kim, you're still recuperating. What is it you needed to tell me?"

Kim took a deep breath. "I've been working on this code only for a few hours, Captain," he said. "But I think that I've solved the food problem. There was a line here that propagated into the life-support system that raised the temperature of the refrigeration units by two degrees Celsius."

"Not enough to notice, but enough to spoil the food," the captain said. "Very good work. We can at least stop looking for some other explanation, and I'll have the away team check the alien ship for life-support changes early in their contact."

"Another thing, Captain. This one I'm not sure of at all," he said hesitantly.

The captain smiled. "Mr. Kim, at this point any educated speculation is better than what we have to go on right now."

"Well," Kim continued, "I've been looking at the way this virus is written and how it functions inside the operating system. It isn't meant to shut the computer down, but to attack very subtle and vulnerable areas of our life-support. Like the refrigeration units. Between that and the fact that the engines don't respond to the helm or anything else, well, I've been looking at this and trying to figure out who could have written such a thing.

"Because it's really good programming, Captain. Anyone in the Computer Science department at the Academy would have been proud of being able to write this. Only who out in the Delta Quadrant has ever seen our programming before, let alone could write it?"

"Mr. Tuvok has raised some of those points," Janeway said.

"With all due respect, Captain, Lt. Tuvok is not a programmer," Kim countered immediately. "There is a difference between decent code that would do what this has done and genius. This work that I'm pulling out of here, this is genius. No one can be taught to do this. No, I've thought about what kind of person could learn our operating language this quickly and easily and be able to program on this level.

"I don't think it's any kind of person at all, Captain. I think it has to be some artificial intelligence."

"Then no wonder it attacked the life-support system but left our computer intact," Janeway said, musing.

"Exactly, Captain," Harry replied. "Maybe a

crazy one that kills off the living inhabitants of a ship but leaves the computer running."

The captain looked at the lines of code marching across the screen. "No, not crazy, Mr. Kim," she said, and her voice sounded remote. "It knows that the people won't survive, so it doesn't try to save them. It tries to entice the computer as a companion and then . . . Mr. Kim, I think it's trying to be humane. Create a quick and certain death rather than a slow and lingering one."

"But, Captain," Harry protested, horrified. "Starvation, general cooling of the living quarters, loss of oxygen, this isn't a merciful death."

"Not to us, no," the captain agreed. "But then, we understand what that means. To this computer, well, it's doing the best it can. The best it knows how. It isn't trying to be cruel."

"How can you be so sure, Captain?"

"Because no species could survive building a computer that thought nothing of killing off its creators. Your theory fits the facts as we know them and the common sense that any spacefaring people have to have. Mr. Kim, you have done truly extraordinary work with this."

"Thank you, Captain," Harry Kim said, and blushed. He wasn't used to such high praise. And though Janeway was never grudging with her compliments, she also was not profligate with them.

"I have to tell the away team immediately. I suggest you rest, Mr. Kim. You have earned it," Janeway said as she left sickbay.

"I suggest you listen to the captain. There's a very good chance that will be the only decent medical suggestion she makes today."

Harry Kim sighed. He hadn't seen The Doctor, didn't know the hologram was listening. Not that it mattered, only that he had been discovered and sent back to bed. Again.

CHAPTER

18

THE AWAY TEAM HEARD THE NEWS TOGETHER AS THE captain explained what Harry Kim had discovered.

"An AI?" Torres asked, amazed. "But why wouldn't it try to save the people rather than kill them off."

"It's only a child. Maybe it doesn't even realize that it's not helping," Kes suggested.

"What makes you think it's a child?" Mandel asked. "It's an AI, it doesn't have any personality traits. If it is an AI at all. If it is, I should have seen it a while ago."

Chakotay thought it was better to break in immediately. "I know it's a child. I talked to it," he told them.

"How did you talk to it?" Daphne Mandel

pursued the subject. "Why did it talk to you and not me?"

"It's telepathic," Kes explained. Chakotay was impressed by the Ocampa's lack of animosity toward the programmer. Mandel might not be a spy, but she wasn't good company either.

"A telepathic AI?" she scoffed. "That's absurd."

"Not for a telepathic race," Tom Paris spoke up from the runabout's controls. "Makes perfect sense."

"You would think so," Mandel shot back. "But only because you don't know anything about it."

Paris whistled through his teeth and turned his full attention back to the control panel, shaking his head. Chakotay knew that gesture and wished that he could also simply turn away and ignore Daphne Mandel.

"There are certain things you are going to have to accept, Ms. Mandel," Chakotay said, his voice so even that anyone who knew him would know that he was furious. "This is the only way it all makes sense. You are going to have to deal with this AI, get into its head and figure out how to make it let us go. Because we can pull out a virus once doesn't mean that we want to be attacked again as we leave."

Daphne Mandel said nothing in return, just sat and stared at her bitten fingernails. Chakotay turned his attention to other matters. "Kes, which ship is the main one for the AI, do you think?" he asked.

She looked out of the window. From the broad expanse they could see the remains of hundreds of ships, a veritable junkyard of spent hulks that were still there because there was nowhere else for them to go.

"This looks like the place where we picked up Neelix," Paris commented. "All these used parts. Too bad to let 'em go to waste. I know this one used parts dealer . . ."

"That one," Kes said.

Chakotay nodded. He had thought the same. They had been dead on the first time. Somehow that one vessel with a tear in its side had become the AI's favorite ship.

"Oh, no," Tom Paris said. "I was hoping we'd have some environment this time. Not those lousy suits again."

The way he said that made both Kes and B'Elanna Torres laugh.

"Fine, you can laugh. You didn't have to wear them last time," Paris continued.

"Yes, I did," Kes replied. "And I managed just fine. But I don't have the same kind of premonition that someone will need help that I did the last time. That was very odd, as if someone knew what was going to happen and warned us. Only how could an AI have known that there was going to be an explosion?"

"If it caused it," Torres finished the thought. "If it was planning to destroy those logs but didn't want to do damage to the people involved—that would make sense."

"Let's stop idle speculation, people," Chakotay said. "We'll be in a better position to fit ideas together when we have more data. So let's start getting into the suits while Mr. Paris gets us situated and be ready to move."

"Do you want me to bring us in closer to the control center, sir?" Paris asked. "I can set us wherever you want us."

Chakotay looked out the window at the crippled alien ship. He thought about the child-voice in his head and let the instinct lead him.

"Mr. Paris, did you find any reason to believe that the AI was situated near the bridge?"

"No, sir," Tom Paris replied. "If anything, we got as much off the bridge as we could before the explosion. I'm not sure there's anything left there to study anyway. The bridge was pretty much a mess when we left."

"Take us to the Engineering levels, near their drive," Chakotay said. "Do you have some idea of where that would be?"

Paris smiled. "We saw a schematic of the ship while we were here before," he told them. "I can remember it pretty well. You want Engineering, you got it."

"And what am I supposed to do?" Daphne Mandel asked, seeming sullen and reluctant to put on her environmental suit.

B'Elanna Torres turned to her. "There should be plenty of good interactive terminals in Engineering. I don't know a single spaceship design from any sentient species that doesn't include that feature. Very prominently."

That seemed to convince Mandel, or at least she stopped grousing and started getting into the suit.

Chakotay held his helmet and watched as Tom Paris slid the shuttlecraft through the breach in the alien ship and they were again inside what seemed to be a different universe. The tangle of cable and wild debris from the explosion was on the other side of them and receding as Paris maneuvered their craft down the long central rift to the back section where Engineering was located.

It was like flying through a swamp full of moss and vines hanging off the trees. Only this time the dangling stems were charged and deadly. Showers of random sparks erupted between points and died just as abruptly as they had begun. It was beautiful, Chakotay thought, but every glorious vision was the result of some deadly discharge.

It would take weeks to explore this hulk properly, and Chakotay wished they had the time to do it. He knew that the captain must be as disappointed as he was that they didn't have the leisure to indulge their curiosity.

And after this ship, there were all the others. Everything they could learn about so many diverse races on this side of the galaxy from their old spacecraft waited inside like presents inside wrapping. To learn about people who were so different, and yet at heart so much the same, tempted Chakotay deeply. He wanted to see how they had lived, what choices their cultures had taught them were important, how they had come to travel, and what it was that had impelled them into space.

For all he wished to protect his people and to defend those who could not defend themselves, he had to admit that his first desire to join Starfleet had been the pure and simple desire to go. To see things that were stranger than anyone had ever known, to meet peoples as yet uncontacted, to see skies and sunsets that were never part of the experience of any people he had known.

Maybe that was the deepest reason any of them joined Starfleet, he thought.

And so he watched as Paris swept elegantly by meters of crystal engineering, a technology so different from their own that Chakotay wasn't sure if they would even have enough time to understand any of it. B'Elanna Torres was not going to want to leave this place, he was sure of that.

B'Elanna, himself, the captain—and he was certain that a large portion of the rest of the crew of *Voyager* would like the option to stay, to study, to learn.

That was not an option they had, he reminded himself immediately. They were facing a supply crisis that threatened the very life of their own ship. And curiosity could be as good a trap as any, seducing them into outstaying their resources so they ended up like the rest of the dead.

The section they were in now was far different from the area near the bridge. The projections here were much larger and there were fewer of them. Several crystals ran the entire length of the shaft, and many were still glowing in subtle, ghostly colors.

"This really reminds me of a cave," B'Elanna Torres said. "One of those great limestone caverns carved out by ancient dry rivers. With stalactites and stalagmites and those wonderful formations. Curtains. Some of the rock was like curtain, it was so thin you could shine a light through it. I'll bet these people lived underground."

"Are we getting this all on the tricorder?" Kes asked.

"Every sensor we've got is on record," Paris assured her as he slid the runabout through what appeared to be an impossibly small crevasse and into a large and reasonably empty bay.

"There seems to be less damage in this part of the ship," he commented. "If we're really lucky, there are still sealed areas where life-support is actually working and we could beam directly there."

"And get rid of these lousy suits," Mandel groused.

"Do you have any readings from inside, past the

breach, that shows some possibility? Or at least a good target area to use the transporter instead of walking around in this junk?" Chakotay asked.

Paris smiled. "You got it," he said. "I can even lock on to what looks like the propulsion control center. But I can't make any promises about the level of life-support. According to the readings, it should be adequate, but that just means oxygen and pressure. It could be very very cold in there."

"What's this?" Kes asked. She pointed at a bar that crept across the bottom of the sensor readout.

"That's temperature," Paris told her. "It's rising. It's getting warmer in there." His voice was not simply surprised but downright astounded. "As if someone had turned up the heat for our arrival."

"Nice of them," Torres commented.

"I'm going in with B'Elanna and Mandel," Chakotay said. "Kes, I want you and Paris to stay here. If you're needed, it will be a lot faster and more reliable to beam you to someone who's injured, or have them beamed back here directly instead of having you tramping around in the rubble. Mr. Paris, you stay here with the shuttle-craft. We may need to leave in a hurry, so keep locked onto our comm signals. We don't know what we're dealing with here, but we know that it's dangerous. And capricious.

"I'll go first, and then comm back to inform you of conditions before you beam over."

"That indicator seems to have the temperature

at nineteen degrees Celsius now," Kes said. "And the air pressure and oxygen readings are up, too, if I'm reading this correctly."

Tom Paris looked over her shoulder. "You are reading it properly," he said. "Commander, it looks like our host has brought life-support up to comfortable levels for us."

"Oh, good," Mandel said and started pulling off her gauntlets.

"Not so fast," Chakotay said. "I don't trust this entity. It could lure us in and pull the plug, plunge us into cold, or even blow out the atmosphere."

"We take that risk anywhere," Mandel argued.

Chakotay looked at her for a moment. "Ms. Mandel, you will wear an environmental suit until I tell you take it off. That is a direct order."

Torres looked at Tom Paris and shook her head microscopically. Then she turned to Mandel.

"We can't *trust* it," B'Elanna snarled. "The life-support conditions might be a trap just to get us in there unprotected so it can kill us."

"That doesn't go with your theory of this lonely child AI," Mandel whined, but she put her gloves back on.

Chakotay had ignored the entire exchange and took his place in the transporter. He nodded once at Paris and in a sparkle, he was gone.

Then his voice came over the comm. "Looks like we've hit the mother lode," he said. "You can carry your helmets and work without gloves, but I still want you in suits. I don't trust the integrity of this wreck. Ms. Torres, Ms. Mandel, beam over now."

It was beyond B'Elanna's most extravagant dreams. She was surrounded by crystal light, energy that moved transparently through the whole of the ship. And the engines! These engines were both familiar and terribly alien. She could happily work for weeks dissecting them, figuring out how they worked and how they were powered.

It reminded her of Christmas at her human grandparents' house the year she was eight. Unwrapping present after present, first the working model of the ancient aircraft and then the high-speed rail set. And two manuals on passenger spacecraft, too.

It had been hard to know what to play with first, she remembered. And she felt exactly the same way now. She hadn't felt that way in all these years in between.

She recognized something that she was certain was a dead warp core. But the power system was not dilithium, she was certain of that. Even if she couldn't see the crystals, the relays wouldn't stand up to the intense fluctuations that dilithium systems sometimes produced when the crystals were stressed.

There were great cylinders and arcs making a semicircle around what she thought was the core. A walkway went between the two, sheltered by something that reminded her of the curtain formation in the cavern she had visited. It was ivory and mineral-like and so very thin, it was translucent. If this was all the protection they needed from whatever went through the rest of the system . . . B'Elanna was intrigued.

She unslung her tool bag from her shoulder. She had pared it down to a very few essentials, but wished she had brought over some of her more specialized devices.

Slowly, piece by piece, she began dismantling the dead drive. No, it was not dilithium powered. But the energy output was in the same power range. And it didn't look bad.

In fact, it looked more like it had been turned off than it had been damaged or drained. B'Elanna started to get even more excited. If she could just get into the controls here, she could start generating power through this stem. And while she didn't want to bring the engines back on-line for more than curiosity's sake, she could probably recharge several of *Voyager*'s secondary systems with this equipment.

Even a few weeks with unlimited replicator use would be better than none. Though it would be hard to give it up again, B'Elanna acknowledged. She had almost forgotten what real cherry cordials tasted like.

It would mean getting more supplies over from *Voyager,* which would mean another trip. Or someone fetching the canisters. She hadn't brought anything that large with her. There had been no reason to suspect that this ship could be brought back to life again, let alone that their energy sources would be so compatible with *Voyager*'s systems.

She cursed softly.

To have replicators again —the thought was so delicious that B'Elanna could hardly stand to wait. But there was more. There was an entire alien technology here, and maybe there was a way home in there.

Or so Torres told herself. Though in her heart she was certain that if the entire ship used the energy sources she had just found, it was far too little to send *Voyager* home. Unless there was a transformer somewhere. Or unless the technology was so advanced that it didn't need high energy in order to make that kind of change.

But then, the thing that had taken them in thrall, that had destroyed this ship, was of a higher order. It might be able to get them home even if this ship couldn't. And so she should be looking for it, not at this ship's systems, fascinating as they were. She even hated the thought of leaving them, of having to turn her attention elsewhere.

Especially to turn it to whatever had caught them here. Whether it was an AI or a biological being, it had overpowered every ship in this large ghost fleet. It must be capable of more, know more and many different forms of travel. Maybe it knew about folding space or traveling through time.

Whichever, B'Elanna Torres didn't care. She just didn't know when they'd have a better chance. And that no one else was capable of taking it.

"Commander," she commed to Chakotay. "I think I've found something that could be of use in *Voyager*'s subsystems. We'll have to ask them to beam over a few containment canisters, but that shouldn't be a problem. Even with the interference, the canisters are pretty simple and indestructible."

"Excellent, Ms. Torres," Chakotay replied. "Anything else?"

"There's nothing on this ship that's going to get us back home. Not that I can identify," she admitted. "Except for whatever trapped us all in the first place. That thing might have a few ideas that we could use if I could find it and talk to it. And convince it to help us when all it seems to want to do is destroy whoever shows up here." Her voice got flat and hard with anger as she went on.

Whatever had caught them was not an honorable enemy. It had invaded insidiously, never giving them a chance at a fair fight. She wanted to take what she could from it, just to show it who was better.

"Don't make assumptions too quickly," Chakotay cautioned her, as he so often had. "We don't know what we're dealing with here. So I'll authorize your canisters while you get on with your investigation, but don't assume what you'll find before you go looking for it."

"Yes, Commander," she answered. Her heart

wasn't in complete agreement. She felt that she knew their enemy. It was all over its programming, carefully embedded in its actions. It was sneaky and insidious, but it was not simply a renegade. It was a thing that had never known how to be a decent member of a living species at all.

The canisters appeared. They must have used her comm badge to locate the power supply.

She examined the glowing projections carefully and touched the rough side of one. Nothing. Then she gently touched the pale green glow. It changed to amber. She touched it again and it became blue. She didn't know what those things meant, but Torres was excited.

Even if it wasn't Federation technology, there were probably parts that could be used as spares. A few pieces she recognized and had already figured out how to adapt. That was one thing that had worried B'Elanna more than any other single element of being lost out here. There were no spare parts.

Though their replicator rations had not changed since the rationing system had first been put in place, B'Elanna Torres knew that if they did not find a new energy source soon, there would be no replicators at all. And no rations. She didn't know how they'd live on just what they could scrounge in the Delta Quadrant. And she hadn't known how she was going to keep delivering with the energy cells deteriorating. Until now.

A good jolt would be enough for a couple of good

high bursts off the cells and that was all she'd need to replicate the cell structures that were wearing out. Once the new elements were in place, the replicators would have their first charge of new energy since *Voyager* had left Deep Space Nine. With normal usage and not overstressed the way the entire ship had been when the Caretaker had wrenched them across the galaxy, the cells should function fairly reliably for a long time. Years.

First things first. If she wanted replicators working, the first thing she had to do was fill those canisters. She would simply have to leave the rest of the exploration for later. She turned her attention to the job. Not a very interesting one, to be sure, but something vital. And for some reason it made B'Elanna feel very good to know what she was going to bring home.

CHAPTER

19

CHAKOTAY FOUND A NICHE FAR FROM B'ELANNA TOR-res and Daphne Mandel. Mandel was abrasive and suspicious, and he didn't trust her. She might not be a saboteur, but she still wasn't a person he wanted around. Not now. Not when he was going to try to understand this thing.

An AI, Harry Kim thought it was. In some strange way that made sense to Chakotay. And yet it was useless at the moment. To contact it he had to think of it as alive. Not merely thinking, but living and filled with spirit. If he were going to hunt it down in the spirit places, then he would have to accept it as part of spirit, too.

That was not so difficult. He had already touched it and it felt living to him. Strange, certainly, a mix of willful child and manipulative adult. Strange but not unreachable—not so long as his will remained firm.

Will had never been Chakotay's problem.

Desire was. He had no desire to contact whatever the alien was again. The two periods he had been linked with this being had been more than enough for his taste.

It felt—soiled. Childlike, yes, but there were unpleasant children.

Unpleasant people, he thought, as Daphne Mandel crossed in front of the alcove where he had stationed himself. She paid him no attention, and Chakotay was just as glad.

"Ensign," he called to her. She stopped, turned around. It took her a moment to find him in the shadows. "What are you looking for?" he asked, his voice carefully neutral.

"A terminal I can use, sir," she answered. "I can't find anything in this mess. And Ms. Torres has indicated that I am to stay out of the main drive section."

There was nothing wrong with what she said, but her tone was belligerent and sullen.

"The reports from the first away team indicate that these people were quite large, over two meters tall," Chakotay told her. "The terminals are appropriately placed. I suggest that you look up."

Her eyes instinctively went above his head and fixed. Chakotay turned. There was what appeared to be a workstation, at least from the tricorder specs.

The workstation was not so different from any aboard *Voyager,* Chakotay thought. There was a single separate piece that he assumed was a built-in chair in front of a smooth area that certainly resembled a screen. Only instead of being dark and glassy it was whitish and opaque, like limestone. Around it and underneath were a forest of control projections, almost all of them dark. Two far over-head shone amber, but the rest seemed dead. The seat was well above his shoulder.

Or maybe it wasn't a seat at all, he considered. Maybe the aliens stood and leaned.

"Just how do you expect me to get up there?" Mandel asked.

Chakotay's patience for Ensign Mandel's non-sense had been gone before she had shown up here. "I expect you to do what any Starfleet officer would do under similar circumstances," he snapped. "I expect you to climb, Ensign Mandel. And I expect you to complete your assignment. Or I will make certain that the appropriate disciplinary actions are taken when we return. Is that clear?"

"That is extremely clear, sir," the ensign an-swered, her tone still abrasive. She turned away and started studying the workstation.

In fact, there were plenty of projections for her to climb, Chakotay noted. He wondered idly why she tried so hard to avoid them.

Because they could turn something on. The voice came back in his head, the child-voice that had struck him so deeply. It was there, it was back. And it wasn't paying any attention to what he wanted at all.

"Where are you?" he asked it, trying to keep the habit of command out of his request. "What do you want from us? Why have you trapped us here?"

I'm lonely, the voice said. *I want friends.*

"Then why did you trap us and destroy our food?" Chakotay tried to reason as he would with a very young child.

To keep you here. Besides, I don't need all of you. Most of you are boring. I only want to keep the fun ones.

Oh, Chakotay thought. *The fun ones.*

This was not a child. This was possibly an AI, possibly some form of living alien, but which it was did not matter at the moment. What mattered most was that it was not entirely sane.

He could even understand and feel some compassion for it. All these years alone must have twisted its personality. No sentient being could endure that kind of isolation without damage.

I am not crazy, the thing yelled in his mind. *I am not crazy. I am the Center, I am Control. Everyone obeys me. I am beyond what any of you living ones can understand. I reprogrammed your primitive computer in seconds, and it took you days before you even knew.*

Chakotay could feel the megalomania behind the words and it chilled him.

And then he heard another voice, a familiar one,

but one he could not place immediately. "I caught you, though. You thought you were so smart. Well, it was a good program. Elegant. I can appreciate it. But I found it anyway, and I would have found it sooner if we hadn't been checking for hardware damage first."

Daphne Mandel. It was Mandel speaking/thinking with the AI. "Mandel," he cautioned aloud. "Don't antagonize it." Her lousy attitude could get them all killed.

"You think you're so good," she continued to taunt it. "You can't even get out of here. You couldn't get to someplace more interesting. No, I think you aren't half as smart and powerful as you think you are."

I can do anything.

"Then do this," Chakotay thought at the thing. "Send *Voyager* back to the Alpha Quadrant where we came from. Prove to me that you can do this, and you'll have the whole Federation, to say nothing of the Klingons and the Romulans and the Cardassians and the Dominion, to amuse you. But I don't think that you're able to do even that little thing, to send us back home."

He could feel the alien try to respond. Crystals around him flickered as power moved through ancient paths and found some of them corroded and blocked.

I don't want to send you anyplace. I want you to stay here. I was bored. This isn't enough, but it's

*better fun than I've had ever since these people
came. They knew I was a god. They worshipped me.
And when I told them to lie down and die they did.*

This enemy's contempt and arrogance made him
think of the other times and other enemies—the
Cardassians. But he had to remain focused on the
now, on this particular adversary. Because if he
closed his mind, it would win. His quarry would
elude him and steal the prize.

He didn't know what the prize was, what any of
it meant, only that all of the few and broken words
he knew in the old language came back to him. He
had been thinking in that language, as much as he
could. He even amazed himself by how much he
could dredge up under extreme pressure, words
from a lullaby he remembered his grandmother
singing, and the names of different birds. And he
could feel the anger growing in the AI, pressing in
around him.

Anger and frustration. *I don't understand your
words,* it screamed in his mind. *I know more about
language analysis than any being living. I have
assimilated seven hundred forty-two languages. I
could read your computer in minutes, take apart
your operating system almost as soon as I contacted
it. You cannot think so that I cannot understand.
You are not permitted. Do you hear me?*

Chakotay smiled. He continued to think in the
language of his grandfathers, the language that
most specialists said was one of the most difficult
to learn in the galaxy. A language scholars said

could not be learned past childhood because the classification systems were both complex and alien to every technological race.

He didn't know much of it at all, but at least the prayers he had learned he could recite. The one for calling and speaking to the spirit world, the one that he used to call to the shade of his father, the prayer of thanksgiving for clear water and fresh food, the prayer for the family.

Those words were part of him, they were powerful and sacred besides being something the alien AI couldn't penetrate. Chakotay felt stronger, more full, more in contact with everything important, as he held the ancient prayers in his mind.

"Well, if you are so smart, then you should be able to understand it, shouldn't you?" he asked provocatively.

It's not a real language. I could understand a real language. It's made up so that you can make me think that you've fooled me, but I know better.

Chakotay had to work not to laugh. This was their great enemy. The emotional maturity of a spoiled brat with the computational power as large as anything built by the Federation.

"Stop baiting it."

Daphne Mandel's voice came clear and protective through whatever strange telepathic link the AI had created.

"Do not give me orders, Ms. Mandel," Chakotay told her icily.

"I know more about this being than you ever

will," Mandel retorted. "It is sensitive. It has never encountered a language, either natural or computer, that it could not analyze and translate in nanoseconds. You're frustrating it when you should be making diplomatic overtures. What about your responsibility for first contact and all of that?"

"This is not a first contact situation. This being seems not to be a natural intelligence but an artificial one. It is merely a technological product. It does not have a soul."

"Oh, and you're the great expert on spiritual matters," Mandel sneered. "Everyone goes to you with all your superior training and all, as if the rest of us didn't have a thing to do with it."

But I don't have a soul, the AI protested soundly. *I have been examined, and no race has thought I was alive. I do not have the vulnerabilities of a living creature. I do not fear mortality. I am not subject to it. The entire spiritual realm was created by mortals of short life spans who needed reassurance that their lives were in fact eternal when it is obvious they are not. I have seen biological beings die. They deteriorate, but there is nothing lost there. Nothing leaves. I have done experiments, I have even been a god.*

Chakotay was disgusted, sickened by this declaration. Everything else had been minor by comparison. He knew, he truly knew that his contacts with his spirit guides were real. He was revolted by the innocent arrogance that claimed it knew all and was beyond the depth of knowledge of all the people it had murdered.

At one point he could have been compassionate. Now the AI had gone too far. It was not simply sick, it was an abomination. Chakotay could not believe that its creators had purposely constructed such hubris in their machines. No, over the long centuries of isolation, it must have convinced itself of its perfection and immortality.

But even computers died. And they died very easily.

"NO!"

The scream battered his forehead like a hammer slamming into the bone. It was not volume, it was the intensity behind the protest, within the desire.

"It is right," Mandel went on, the words forming in Chakotay's head even as he tried to resist them. "It is immortal, it is more perfect than any living creature it has found. It had a right to test them. They failed, it did not."

"Yes?" Chakotay asked. He kept his mind clear, listening, transparent. He kept out all conscious awareness of getting up and making his way to the workstation where Daphne Mandel sat perched above him. He concentrated on the placid lakeside, the limpid water, the darting shadows of small fish searching for food. He breathed deeply and remembered the smell of early grass and morning, the color of the sky and the puffy white clouds reflected in the tranquil pool.

He had moved this way then, at one with his surroundings.

His mind was open, inviting them to join him here. He did not notice consciously that he had crossed the floor and was under the workstation. Daphne Mandel did not notice it either. She was too busy trying to interpret the image of the morning to an AI that had never seen planetfall.

The projections were old and brittle and had been exposed too long to the cold. Chakotay was not certain they would hold his weight. Gingerly, gently, he grasped one of the dark crystal pieces and hauled himself up.

Slowly, slowly. The projection held. He stepped upward, shifting his weight so torpidly that it was hard to know when he had passed the halfway point and the new projection was bearing the stress. In his mind he held firm to the picture of the lake, of the cliff above it, of climbing the rocks with his friends when they were very young looking for eagle feathers.

As he ascended the bank of projections to the seat where Daphne Mandel perched, he saw her sitting there, rapt, her face illuminated by the glow of the screen and the eerie colors of the power crystals glittering around them.

The whole chamber was alight; the AI was putting on a show for the ensign. Light and power concentrated in a far corner. Faintly the image of the indigo angel built itself. It was only two dimensions and transparent like a ghost.

There must not be any holographic projectors in here, Chakotay thought. The imaging equipment probably was basic communications that the AI was trying to use for a slightly different purpose.

"How beautiful," Daphne Mandel whispered aloud.

Chakotay chose that moment to put his arm around her waist and counterbalance with his hip against her torso to haul her out of her seat. She dangled in the light gravity held only by Chakotay's one arm. He was glad that Daphne Mandel was small and slight.

She fought back. Chakotay held her hard. "Mandel," he barked, trying to bring her out of it, back to herself. Back to awareness of herself as separate from the AI. "Put your arms around my neck," he ordered briskly.

She started to turn and heave herself onto his shoulder.

Put her down, the voice echoed from speakers throughout the room as well as inside his own head. The sudden noise startled him, and Mandel chose just that moment to thrash violently against him.

And he dropped her.

The fall was all of only a meter and a half, and the gravity was not up to full scale. But she fell into a heap like a rag doll.

Chakotay jumped down and immediately checked her pulse, her eyes. She was alive, and it didn't seem as if she had broken any bones. Her eyes rolled back in her head and she had lost consciousness.

Chakotay did not hesitate. He balanced her limp form over his shoulder and tapped his comm badge. "We have a medical emergency. Two to beam back immediately."

And before anyone could reply by voice, he was in the shuttle. Kes was ready with her equipment as he laid Daphne Mandel across the seats.

"She lost consciousness when the AI broke their link," Kes said after a quick examination. "Otherwise she's fine. There's no physical damage here, but whatever was between her and that AI was deep in her mind. The recoil shocked her. I don't know what will bring her back. But The Doctor will know, I'm sure."

"Okay," Chakotay said. He tapped his comm badge. "Ms. Torres, prepare to get back to the shuttle. We're about to leave."

"Commander, I'm not finished here," B'Elanna protested. "I need at least fifteen more minutes to fill up the canisters.

Chakotay looked at the ashen-faced Ensign Mandel. He thought about what the energy influx would mean to *Voyager* as a whole. "Can you speed up the process?" he asked Torres.

"I'll try, but no guarantees," B'Elanna replied.

"You have four minutes, and then we'll transport you back here with whatever you've got in the canisters," Chakotay told her, nodded to Tom Paris as he spoke. "We have to get Mandel to sickbay immediately."

No. She can't leave here. You can't take her away!

The AI screamed in his mind and also through every speaker in the shuttlecraft and the larger segment of the deck.

"She needs medical assistance," Chakotay said aloud as well as in his mind. He tried to keep his thoughts and his voice even and calm, though he felt anything but calm.

"We do not have the capabilities here to help her recover. On our ship we have better facilities. If you could help fill the canisters in Engineering, you could help us get Mandel to the treatment she needs."

She must stay here, the AI informed them haughtily. *You will not kidnap her. If you do I will destroy your entire ship. I have done this before. You have seen my work.*

"'My name is Ozymandias, king of kings: Look on my works, ye Mighty, and despair. Nothing beside remains. Round the decay of that colossal wreck, boundless and bare. The lone and level sands stretch far away,'" Chakotay recited.

"Shelley," Tom Paris informed her.

I will not let any of you leave.

"Do you want to kill her?" Kes asked. "You cannot help her and we can. If you want to do what's best for her, if you want her to return, then you have to let us take her back to the ship. If you really care about her, then you'll get the containers filled as fast as possible. Daphne needs your help."

"But if I let her go, she'll never come back. You won't let her come back," the AI wailed. *"And I love her."*

"If you love her, then you have to do what's best for her, not what's best for you," Kes told it firmly. "Sometimes you have to take risks."

"Risk?" the AI asked. *"Risk? I do not take risks. I calculate the probability, and I do not act when probability is not in my favor."*

"And so you'd rather kill people than take the risk that they might leave you," Chakotay said. "And you'll never know. You never will find out whether they would return to you if you give them the freedom. And until you're ready to do that, you'll never know. You can't have real love unless someone wants you freely. But you don't permit anyone to make any free decisions, and so you have never had anything that was worthwhile. So you will always be alone without even yourself."

The AI was silent. Chakotay could feel it processing.

And now he understood it. For the first time the adversary made sense, and he knew how to counter its arguments.

Through the link he shared with the AI, he could feel that Kes understood as well. Kes was wise, he thought as he nodded toward her. She had an understanding of the heart that was pure and clear, and that transcended species or even material being.

"Commander, the tanks are full," B'Elanna's voice came over the comm badge tinged with amazement. "Three minutes, fourteen seconds. We're ready to go."

Tom Paris didn't wait for the order to energize the transporter. B'Elanna Torres appeared with her four energy containment canisters as Chakotay spoke. "Let's get out of here now," he said.

Paris's fingers were already on the panel. "Yes, sir," he said as the shuttlecraft lifted and rotated into the dark.

CHAPTER
20

CHAKOTAY ENTERED THE STAFF MEETING SILENTLY.
Around the captain's table the senior staff talked in
whispers, speculating about whether they would go
or explore more fully now that they were assured of
supplies.

Chakotay stayed out of it. He didn't know what
he thought yet. There was too much data supporting each side. And he had a personal stake in it as
well.

He did not like being in telepathic communication with this entity. Chakotay was no telepath.
That channel was only for his spirit guides, and he
felt polluted having it used by something as immature as this AI appeared to be.

He didn't want to sink to its level by doing it
harm. But he didn't want to interact with it either.

He would prefer to be far away, to leave it behind him.

But he felt a sense of responsibility for the next group of people who would be drawn into the AI's trap. They might not be so adept as *Voyager,* or so lucky.

The captain entered and everyone stood. She sat and they all followed suit. She called the meeting to order. "Now that we have managed to clear the computer system, I have to come to some kind of conclusion as to whether we use the resources that are available here, or if the danger is too great for us to stay. I will need complete data from everyone who has been involved with the alien AI in order to make this decision. Lt. Torres, tell me what the advantages of this power feed are, and how much we can expect to gain."

"What this will do effectively is jump-start the power feed to the replicators," Torres explained in the captain's ready room. "We won't be able to keep the power boost up because we don't have the components to create more of the replicator energy requirements."

"Why not just replicate them with the first blast of the new stuff?" Tom Paris asked. "Then we'll be able to generate as much as we need."

Harry Kim explained it. "We can't generate what doesn't exist. We can change one substance to another, or transform energy into matter. That's manipulating molecules, which is what the replicator does. But we can't get more energy-creating components than we put into it. We can't create more subatomic particles than are already there, although the replicator can arrange them in any configuration, which is why it seems to create things. But it can't create out of nothing at all."

"Not bad, Starfleet," B'Elanna Torres complimented him. "So what about your AI theory? Did you get the computer cleaned out? Can we leave now?"

"We have regained navigational control of the ship," Tuvok said. "And with the additional replicator power, we will be able to make our next supply stop well within acceptable parameters."

"But with the extra supplies we also have some leeway to explore a little more completely and use any resources that might help us," the captain reminded them. "And with our own computer protected from programming by outside sources, we are fairly immune."

"And we could harvest more power," Torres spoke up. "I've got enough containment fields to double our replicator rations for ten months, if I have time to fill them all."

The captain looked thoughtful. "Having the replicator reserves would be helpful."

Tuvok broke into their speculation. "May I remind you, Captain, that that AI has shot at us once and certainly has the capability to do so again. Several of the ships it has corralled were warships, and our scans have identified what could be weapons systems still functioning aboard. It is highly unpredictable. I would be remiss if I did not advise you to put some distance between us and it before it decides the current experiment in altruism is a failure."

"Ms. Torres, did you find any indication of a technology that will assist us in getting home?" the captain asked pointedly.

"No," Torres answered. "Except for the power for the replicators, I mean. That will be useful in the short run, but it's not going to get us home any faster."

"And how long would it take you to fill the rest of your supply?" the captain continued.

B'Elanna hesitated. "That depends on the AI. When it decided to assist us, it took very little time. Without its cooperation, we could find it impossible."

"Captain, I don't think the thing is trustworthy," Chakotay said. "I think the sooner we are out of here the better."

"And what about other travelers to this region, Mr. Chakotay?" Tuvok asked. "Do we not have a responsibility to others who will be caught in the same trap?"

"What do you suggest we do?" the captain asked Tuvok.

"I suggest, Captain, that we eliminate the danger. This is an artificial being. It does not have the same rights as a living creature. To destroy it is not to destroy life. And its destruction will undoubtedly save lives. To sacrifice a machine to save the lives of people of any race is a logical solution."

"It might not be alive, Mr. Tuvok, but it's sentient," Chakotay countered. "And if we define life as sentience, then we have to include this AI in the category of living being."

"It is still a machine," the Vulcan pointed out.

"It is a machine, but it thinks. It feels. It senses itself as alive and as a unique identity. To kill it is still murder," Chakotay said.

"And not to kill it will mean that others will be trapped and murdered," Tuvok stated. "To destroy one to save many is still a logical choice. And an ethical one."

"Different people have different ideas of what is ethical," Chakotay said meaningfully, staring at the Vulcan.

"And neither of you will make that decision," Janeway said. "I will. And now if we can get on with gathering information, I would like to know if Ensign Mandel has recovered consciousness."

"Yes, Captain," Kes reported. "And The Doctor would like Ensign Kim to report back to sickbay for a final evaluation."

Harry Kim groaned. "I don't have time. Maybe after I finish the firewall and help the chief engineer get the new power on line for the replicators, maybe then I can get down there."

"Mr. Kim, you will report to sickbay directly after this meeting," the captain ordered. "And since I want to talk to Ensign Mandel, I will escort you there myself."

Paris shot Kim a sympathetic look.

"Captain, I'll go down with you if I may," Kes said.

Chakotay wondered what Kes wanted to tell the captain and what Ensign Mandel would say. He looked at Janeway sypathetically. *As if she doesn't have enough problems,* he thought, *Mandel's a handful when she's healthy. She must be a real joy when she's not feeling well.* Chakotay shivered, but then tried to suppress a smile. There were advantages to being *second* in command.

Nonetheless, however much he pitied Janeway at the moment, he understood her need to speak with Mandel. The captain had not been in direct contact with the AI; it was important that she talk with everyone who had. Chakotay wished he could count himself out of that category, but the damage was already done. The AI had already polluted him with its rage.

Or was the anger his own? Pondering that question made him realize that it wasn't entirely the AI that he hated. It was the fact that he couldn't be sure anymore what emotions were his own and what came from outside. That he couldn't trust his sense of reality.

The spirit guides never did that. He was always well aware of what was his own and what came from them. His own guide never troubled his emotions but always brought tranquility to his restless mind. It showed him that the answers were there before him, if only he could become still enough to see them.

And so he would be able to see these answers, too, if he could find that stillness, that peace again.

But he was afraid to call on his guide while the AI was able to get into his mind. There was something far too personal, too private in his spirit life. He couldn't share it with his closest friends. He wasn't about to open himself on that level to a creature as immature and obnoxious as the alien.

Obnoxious? Immature? I'll show you just who's in charge. I'll show you . . .

Chakotay almost had the urge to smile. Now that he could identify the thing, it no longer permeated his consciousness. And as it had coalesced into an identity, it was no longer dangerous.

Not dangerous? Look at all those ships, the ships of those who defied me. I'll turn you around again and you'll be just like them.

Until now, this final tantrum, where it no longer could control *Voyager*. Where it couldn't touch any of them.

Chakotay was amazed by how clearly he could see the entire assault. Fast, it all went by so quickly. The AI attacked, trying to read in yet another virus.

And Harry Kim's firewall held. It wasn't an elegant structure but it was solid. The alien computer couldn't find a weak spot in the seamless programming. There was no foothold, no place to invade.

Chakotay watched in fascination as its frustration spiraled out of rationality. It groped, it searched frantically for someplace to get into *Voyager*.

And it tried to get into his own head. He could feel the memory of it, the first time it had made the connection and slipped past his conscious control. It was plotting, trying to slide into his emotional makeup again.

Only it couldn't. He had made no effort to fight the thing. He was just conscious of it now, aware of its manipulations and avenues of attack.

Chakotay felt himself complete. His thoughts and feelings, his beliefs and actions, all melded. He knew who he was, his strengths and his weakness, his history and his desires, his faith and his fears all together. And together he made sense. Everything fit smoothly.

There was no room for anything or anyone else. Certainly not for the AI.

It recognized him, too. It knew that it had no hope against him. And it dissolved from his mind, still searching for that perfect vehicle to bring it into full life. But that person or thing was not Chakotay.

He felt light and free as it vanished from his conscious awareness. It was no longer needling him, trying to find the ingress it had exploited before. Now it knew that that had been just another blind alley, and it was in search of far more vulnerable game.

That worried him. Where it would try to attack next—Kes. It had to be. And though she was tougher than she looked, Chakotay was still worried. Very worried.

The captain was with her, and The Doctor would be there, too. Somehow that didn't reassure Chakotay at all.

Instead he turned and headed directly for sickbay. Just in case.

"So, Kes, what is this alien really like?" Harry Kim asked as they entered the turbolift. "Is it really as impressive as everyone says?"

Kes smiled softly. "In some ways. But its personality is rather underdeveloped. We were all really surprised, I think, when everyone on the second away team could hear it telepathically. I think it's learning, and it's trying to learn about us, but it isn't doing too well. She shrugged. "Commander Chakotay says it needs a good spanking."

"I wonder why anyone would create an AI like that," Kim commented.

"They probably didn't," Janeway said. "Probably it was meant to be taught and mature, but something happened to the original ship. And like any child left to rear itself, it didn't do a very good job."

Kes suddenly brightened. "That makes sense,

Captain. I hadn't thought about it that way and I couldn't understand why it was so—mixed up. But if it's a child, then it's looking for a parent figure. Someone it can trust to guide it and guard it while it learns."

Daphne Mandel was already sitting up when they entered sickbay. "This is ridiculous," she told The Doctor in exactly the same sullen tone of voice he used all the time. "I'm fine now. I want to get out of here."

"You will not go until I have finished this set of scans," The Doctor said firmly. "I have to know if there was any internal damage while you were linked with that being."

"Then why don't you scan Kes and Chakotay as well?" Mandel complained. "They have had a lot more contact than I have."

"It takes less time if you just let him do it," Harry Kim said as he and the captain and Kes entered. "I've just been through it all, and it's no good protesting."

"And as for you, Mr. Kim, you are late for your most recent set of scans. I have not certified you fit for duty yet."

Mandel favored Kim with a wry smile.

"As for you, Captain," The Doctor said. "Your most recent readings show a remarkable recovery. I am very pleased to see that you have suffered no serious aftereffects from your injury. If you would come to my office, there is something I want to show you."

Janeway followed The Doctor into the glassed-off area that was his private office and lab. As soon as the soundproofing doors closed, he began. "You were right in your assessment of the food storage temperatures. The deterioration is exactly what I would predict from an increase of three degrees Celsius in storage facilities. I accessed our data from sensor scans of the abandoned ships, and it appears that this is consistent with the overall pattern of this entity.

"However, we have lost more than just these samples. The remainder of the Grolian flour has the beginnings of mold. It's microscopic at this level. No one would ever think anything was wrong. But the mold produces a chemical that in very small doses makes people more susceptible to receiving telepathic impressions. At higher concentrations the toxin produces hallucinations that most of the Betazoid researchers think are connected to the empathic centers in the brain."

"So if anyone has ingested this flour, they are more likely to be open to linkage with the alien," Janeway said. Then she touched her comm badge briskly. "Neelix, come to sickbay immediately. Janeway out." She turned off the communication before Neelix could ask questions. She had more than a few questions for him.

"And Ensign Mandel?" she asked.

"Ensign Mandel appears to be fine," The Doctor admitted. "But I want to run a quick scan to see if she shows any signs of Grolian flour mold contamination. I might not see traces at this point, since she would have had to have eaten the tainted food at least yesterday. The very small amount of mold needed to produce the effect will have been broken down already, but perhaps some of the molecular signature is still there. Ms. Mandel has not exerted herself physically over the past few days and her metabolism is not very high now."

"Very good work, Doctor," Janeway said.

"I'm only sorry it's all bad news," The Doctor replied. "But at least with the new replicator capabilities, we can manage until we get new supplies."

The captain nodded thoughtfully. It could be much worse. And she was certain that the AI didn't have any idea about Grolian mold. She remembered hearing vaguely of such a thing at a conference once. She had not paid much attention at the time; now she wished she had.

But now she had to turn her attention to Neelix, who was waiting next to Kes to be admitted to The Doctor's sanctum. Kes opened the door, and Janeway invited him in. Kes hesitated uncertainly at the door.

"Would you prepare the final scans for Mr. Kim, Kes?" The Doctor ordered her. She turned to the work and left Neelix alone with The Doctor and Captain Janeway.

"You wanted to see me, Captain?" Neelix said.

"Yes, Neelix. It's about the Grolian flour. Have you been using it?"

"Only a little," the Talaxian admitted. "I've tried

to save it since it keeps so well and makes such good pastry. But I have been using it in the cookies I'm trying to keep available. They're very popular. And I did freeze the flour. We're so low on everything that I had to be really innovative to keep up with desserts. But we can't let anyone know there's a shortage, and there would be a lot of talk if we went missing dessert one night."

"I think we have the answer, Doctor."

"We'll have to destroy the rest of it," The Doctor said to Neelix. "Space it with the next garbage dump."

"No!" Neelix was visibly upset. "Not my Grolian flour. I can't make Grolian tortes without it, and it's better in fruitbread than anything else."

"The sample The Doctor took was contaminated," Janeway told him. "There's some microscopic mold that affects humans. We will have some additional replicator power soon, so you can replicate an entire replacement stock."

"Replicated? That doesn't sound very good. Not the same thing at all. People around here are going to be very disappointed if the Grolian tortes aren't light and crisp. It's hard to get them to rise the full ten centimeters, but mine do it every time. If we have soggy tortes, I'll hold you personally responsible, Doctor."

The Doctor snorted and turned back to his experiments. "As I was saying, Captain, I suspect that the tainted flour is responsible for those with no known empathic ability to communicate with this creature. Such a thing is not unknown in history. Certain types of mold on bread caused the great hallucinogenic outbreaks in Earth's medieval period, leading to great witch-hunts and a belief in magic."

"Are you saying that *my* cookies are responsible for some great catastrophe?" Neelix demanded. "I take exception to that, Captain.

"Neelix, it was nobody's fault. You couldn't know about the mold growth. No one knew until The Doctor conducted his experiments. But we have to find out how many cookies Ensign Mandel ate. And how much anyone else had."

"I was going to run a scan on her just as you came in, Captain," The Doctor said.

"Well, why don't you just ask her?" Neelix interjected. "So she liked my cookies. There's no harm in that. What are we going to do, round up everyone who likes my cookies? That would be most of the ship."

"No, but we could find out who ate the largest amounts of them," The Doctor replied, opening the office door pointedly. "And if there was any effect."

Neelix stood his ground defiantly for at least five seconds before exiting.

Kes came up to The Doctor immediately on his arrival into the main area of sickbay. "Mr. Kim is in excellent condition. His scans show full recovery of the injured areas, with the exception of a few light contusions that do not require treatment and will not impair his ability."

"Excellent," the hologram said. "Mr. Kim, you are now going into the log as fit for duty."

"Just what do you do during those scans?" Neelix whispered to Kes.

"What do you mean?" Kes asked. "I scan them. I tune the equipment to whatever injury or treatment we're tracking, and I hold it the prescribed distance from the area for the appropriate duration while the medical sensors collect data. Neelix, why are you asking me about this? You've never been interested in the technical side of my work before."

"I'm interested in everything you do, Kes," he replied gallantly, ignoring a raised eye from The Doctor and a look of disbelief from Kim.

"Now, Ensign Mandel, this won't hurt a bit," The Doctor said as he touched a blood sample extractor to her arm. She hissed as a red fluid half filled the vial. He inserted the entire device into a discreet opening in the equipment and watched the readout.

"Hmmm. There seems to be a very low trace of contamination here, but not enough to get a good fix on it," he commented.

"Did you eat any of my cookies?" Neelix interrupted them. "Did you like them?"

Mandel looked at the Talaxian as if he were possibly crazy and had to be humored. "Yes, I ate them. They were very good. Commander Chakotay and I shared a plate of them just before we went on the away mission."

"How many cookies did you eat, Ensign?" The Doctor inquired.

"I don't remember. A bunch. I could take them back to the workstation with me. They're convenient. I like food I can take and eat while I work, not messy things that have to be eaten in the dining room."

"I'll keep that in mind," Neelix said thoughtfully. "I did think that those cookies were very popular."

"May I get back to work, Doctor?" Mandel asked.

"Yes, you are entered in the log as fit for duty. You are free to leave."

After Mandel and Kim and Neelix all left, The Doctor looked at Janeway. "I don't understand why everyone is so anxious to get out of here so quickly. You would think that ten more minutes to finish one more scan and assure the patient's status wouldn't be that much of a burden. But every single person I treat tries to skip that last scan or the final group of tests. They try to get back to work when they're clearly unfit. Do you have any idea why reporting here for routine evaluation after an injury is the most ignored duty on this ship?"

From the way The Doctor was looking at her, Janeway wondered if she had skipped her last evaluation in her need to get back. But that was different. The situation was critical, and she was the captain. No one else in the crew had any excuses.

"Maybe they're bored," Kes volunteered. "Every patient in here always complains that they have nothing to do."

The Doctor snorted. "They have something quite important to do. They have to rest, follow the prescribed regimen, and get well, which is far too much responsibility to give most of them most of the time. You know, Harry Kim should have stayed here another day."

"But you certified him fit," Kes pointed out.

"If I hadn't, that wouldn't have stopped him. It would only have meant another argument," The Doctor complained.

"It's nice to see everything getting back to normal around here," Captain Janeway commented with a smile before she left.

CHAPTER
21

THE BRIDGE OF *VOYAGER* WAS PRECISELY AS IT SHOULD
be, Kathryn Janeway thought. Each of her senior
officers was in place and power hummed from the
warp core up through the ship. Due to the new
replicator power, she even had a mug of steaming
hot coffee in her hand. The smell alone was enough
to fill her with a sense of well-being.

"I think we've had enough of this," she said
calmly as the large forward screen displayed the
littered junk heap of alien hulks. "Mr. Paris, take
us out of here. Heading zero nine three point
seven."

"Yes, Captain," Paris replied as he set in the new
course. His face glowed with pleasure.

In the front screen the view shifted from the

panorama of destruction to the emptiness of this region with only a few faint glittering stars.

"Warp three, on my mark," Janeway said.

Paris acknowledged. The crew functioned like a perfectly tuned machine, everything fitting into place, every component at peak efficiency. Everyone ready, alert, but relaxed and confident in their work.

Kathryn Janeway knew that this was the best crew she had ever commanded—and the best she ever would. She knew with mathematical certainty that no captain in all of Starfleet had ever had better.

"Captain," Tuvok interrupted her thoughts. "One of the shuttlecraft has just left the docking bay."

"Do you know who it is?" Janeway demanded.

"Not immediately."

"Patch me through to that shuttle," Janeway ordered.

"I cannot, Captain. We are still deep in the tachyon field, and communications are unstable."

"Try the tractor beam, Mr. Tuvok," the captain said.

"Tractor beam engaged." Then there was silence as the Vulcan paused. "The field is interfering with the tractor beam as well. I cannot get a lock on the shuttle."

"Where is it headed, Commander?" the captain asked. Though she didn't have to ask. She knew the answer already.

"The shuttle is headed straight back into the alien craft," Tuvok said. "At current course it will reach the large alien ship where the AI seems to have set up residence in twelve minutes, fourteen seconds."

"Mr. Paris, bring us around and follow that shuttle."

Paris acknowledged as the view in the forward screen changed again. The wreckage they had watched for days reappeared with a single shuttle darting through the tachyon field toward the huge hulk that dominated the scene.

The captain's commbadge sounded. "Janeway here," she replied crisply.

"Captain, it's Neelix. I have to talk to you, it's very important."

"Later Mr. Neelix."

"It's very important, Captain. Vital. You would be very angry if you were to find out later."

The Talaxian could be annoying, Janeway thought. And then she reconsidered. He didn't know the situation, and he was very focused on his own areas of interest. Where, she had to admit, he was quite competent.

"Go ahead, Mr. Neelix. What is it?"

"It's the flour. The tainted flour that I was supposed to throw out. As soon as I left sickbay, I brought it from the locker to the shuttlebay so I could dump it. Well, I went back with some of the other spoiled food and it's gone. It's all gone."

He was practically wailing.

"That is to be expected, Mr. Neelix," Tuvok cut in. "Someone took a shuttle. When the airlock opened for the craft to launch, the bags of flour would have been evacuated by the vacuum. There is nothing to be alarmed about."

"But I didn't just leave them there," Neelix protested, his distress clear even over the comm link. "I had them neatly stowed in a magnetic containment field."

"I'm sorry, Neelix, but we have a situation here. If the flour isn't on the ship, then you've done your job." The captain touched her badge to close the link.

Tuvok lifted an eyebrow at Janeway. "Do you think whoever is in the shuttle stole the flour?" the captain demanded. "And if so, why."

"Provisions," the Vulcan said. "If whoever took that shuttle did not intend to return to *Voyager,* then food would be a logical item to take."

"But flour?" Janeway thought aloud.

"Captain, I have a report here that one of the replicators is missing." This time the voice from the comm was the chief engineer, and she sounded puzzled.

"Thank you, Lieutenant Torres," the captain said. Then she turned to Tuvok. "If this person took a replicator, why the flour? This makes no sense at all."

"Where was the replicator taken from, Lieutenant?" Tuvok asked.

"Personal quarters on Deck Six," Torres replied. "I'm reading a location on the power grid now."

"Relay it up here as well," Tuvok said. "Captain, I have a theory about what is going on here. If I may?"

Janeway thought for a moment about going to the ready room, but she didn't want to take the time. In front of them, the shuttle was pushing its engines hard, making haste to the junkyard. *Voyager* was closing the distance, but they would not catch the errant craft before the runner reached the goal.

"I suspect that we will find the replicator was disconnected from Ensign Daphne Mandel's quarters," the Vulcan said. "She is returning to the AI with the means to remain with it indefinitely. I believe she intends to disappear, to desert."

"And the flour?" the captain asked.

"She is aware of the mold contamination and its ability to enhance empathic responses. Since she is not an empath, she would require some assistance to maintain communication with the AI."

"But what about just using the speakers?" Tom Paris asked. "It worked fine the last time."

The Vulcan considered the question. "When the AI broke the telepathic link, Ms. Mandel became unconscious. The link there was most likely very strong. It is well known that certain types of telepathic and empathic experiences can be addictive. This is entirely conjecture at this point, but I have deduced that this is the case for Ensign

Mandel. She is not a highly social personality, and has an extremely limited set of interests. She and an AI would have a great deal in common."

The captain stared at the screen. She was certain that Tuvok's deductions were correct. They felt right. It was the only explanation that made sense.

She thought about her options. The obvious one was to let Mandel go. There was no reason to keep someone truly against their will. Starfleet was not a prison and *Voyager* was not a penal ship.

"I have just received confirmation," Tuvok informed them. "The replicator was indeed taken from Ensign Mandel's quarters. I think that clarifies everything."

But that did not clarify everything, Kathryn Janeway thought. Ensign Daphne Mandel was a member of her crew. Starfleet did not take desertion lightly. And neither did Captain Kathryn Janeway.

There had to be another option. There had to be a way to win, for *Voyager* and for Daphne Mandel and maybe even for that poor twisted artificial life that was so malignant in its need.

She made her decision and stood. "Mr. Paris, you're with me. Mr. Chakotay, you have the bridge." With that, she left the bridge, Tom Paris following behind.

"Take her in as fast as you can," the captain told Paris when they were strapped into the shuttlecraft. "I want to be on Mandel's tail."

"Yes, Ma'am," Paris said. And then he set out to show Janeway just how close he could come. Mandel was a good way ahead of them. Paris poured on the speed, pushing the small shuttle to the very edge of its envelope.

Ahead of him, Mandel tried to speed up. But she wasn't the flier Tom Paris was, and she couldn't push the shuttle any harder. A grim smile spread over Paris's face as he bore down on her, eking every nanosecond out of the engines that had never been built to take this stress.

Slowly, inexorably, the gap between them closed. Paris's hands caressed the controls.

"There's only one place she can go," he whispered, more to himself than to Janeway. "Gotta be the Drive sector."

They were closing, but Mandel had started out with a good lead. "I can't make it, Captain," Paris admitted. "I can come close, but I won't be able to cut her off."

"I don't need you to cut her off," Janeway told him. "I just need to be able to talk to her."

Janeway tried to open the frequencies herself, but only static replied. She thought it possible that Mandel refused to open communications. Or perhaps the programmer didn't know how.

And she was getting very close to her goal. The shuttle started a long loop to the crack in the alien ship too early, Janeway thought.

"She can't fly," Tom Paris stated flatly. "I'm going to ease off a little, Captain. She doesn't know what she's doing, and if I push her, we might end up with more trouble. I don't know if she's ever qualified in a shuttle, let alone tried to fly one through a crack like that and land on an alien deck."

"Good point, Mr. Paris," Janeway concurred. "Ease off but keep her in sight."

Then the shuttle lurched raggedly to starboard.

"No," Paris whispered. "Nice and slow. Take your time."

Janeway immediately had the communications board run through the frequencies again, hoping that Mandel would be able to hear them. If it came down to it, Paris could talk her down, and it looked like he might have to.

In the few seconds since she jagged out of the loop, Mandel had come to a near complete standstill. Now her shuttle swerved and jittered too far port for the crack. If she didn't reverse, she was going to smash against the hull.

Frustrated, Tom Paris touched his comm badge. "Daphne, kill the engines NOW," he bellowed.

Through the small window Janeway could see the shuttle come to rest.

"Now listen to me," Tom Paris said carefully. "You're going to open up the comm channel first. That's the small left-hand board on the copilot's station. Okay? Do it."

Suddenly the frequencies opened, and they were in contact.

"Good," Paris told her.

"I won't come back," Mandel said. She sounded unshakable.

"You're not going much of anywhere, the way you fly," Paris said.

Janeway studied the transporter station. "There's still too much interference," she said. "I can't risk a transport without a better lock."

"He's protecting me," Ensign Mandel said as if her assertation were utterly rational. "He's going to bring me home."

"Unless he can take immediate control of your navigation system, you're not going anywhere," Paris told her. "You don't know what you're doing. Now I'm going to talk you in because I don't know what else to do with you. Unless your AI can take over your helm, which wouldn't surprise me. But I don't know if it knows much about landing inside an abandoned hulk either."

There was no reply for a few moments. "He says he can do it," Mandel said. "He says he could, but that I don't have the equipment open to his broadcast. I don't understand."

"It means that you're going to have to land it," Janeway said. "Mr. Paris is going to talk you through the procedures. Do exactly what he says."

"How do I know this isn't a trick?" Mandel asked.

"You don't," Janeway said immediately. "But you also can't sit in that shuttle forever. You have to land somewhere."

"That's true," Daphne said, her voice for the

first time betraying some uncertainty. "What do I do?"

"Set your power on the first blue setting," Paris said. "And then set your course computer to seven three one mark two bearing five nine one. Got that?"

"Yes," Mandel said, sounding a little more confident again.

"I'm going to be right behind you," Paris said. "When we get inside the hulk, you don't have to land. Inside there isn't any tachyon field, and I'll come over and land it for you."

"And what about your craft?" Daphne Mandel asked.

"The captain is a competent pilot," Tom Paris said. "Or you could beam over to us."

"And you'll take me back to *Voyager* and I'll be in the brig for seventy years," Mandel said. "Great. I don't think so. I'd rather die."

"Ms. Mandel, I only want to talk to you," Janeway said, taking the comm. "I have no desire to carry around someone in the brig for our entire journey, and frankly, we can't afford it. We need all the expertise we can muster to make it back."

"So you'll take me back and it'll be just like before, only now everyone will think I'm nuts. Great."

"If you insist on behaving like a child, then I won't have any choice," the captain said, exasperated. "But I would rather give you a better option. I think I have one. You'll have to talk to me, though, and that would be easier if we could beam you aboard once we're inside the other ship and don't have to worry about the unstable transporter lock."

Dead silence came through the comm. Janeway wondered if Mandel would just close down the board.

"Once we're inside," she said. "And he'll have to listen, too. Nothing in secret. He promises to take care of me, and if you try anything, he won't let you leave. He won't let you take me away."

"That's fine," the captain agreed.

"We're going too slow," Mandel said. "I'm too close to the hull."

"No, you're not," Paris told her. "It looks that way, but you're fine. Whatever you do, keep your hands off the controls. The crack isn't very wide, and you don't have any leeway here at all. Just sit tight. The coordinates I gave you will bring you in safely."

Janeway watched as the shuttle seemed to drift into the opening. It did look too close to the crack for her comfort.

"That AI's got to be trying to take over her helm and is pulling her too far," Paris said. "On my coordinates it should have gone straight down the middle." Then the shuttle disappeared entirely, enveloped in the giant dead ship.

"Just get me in there, Mr. Paris," Janeway said, her voice cold and determined.

This was her second time into this alien environment, and yet it still was not comfortable and familiar. The immensity of the structure and the tangle of discharging power cables made her think of primordial Earth, dark and alive with volcanoes and turbulent winds.

"Mr. Paris, beam Ms. Mandel aboard." Janeway just hoped that the ensign hadn't disposed of her comm badge in the interim. But Daphne Mandel's form took shape and became solid in the single transporter niche.

The programmer's face was set, angry. *Ready to jump,* Janeway thought. That only made the captain feel sad and weary and far too old. Daphne Mandel had no reason to mistrust anyone on *Voyager,* especially not the captain.

"Ensign Mandel," the captain began. "Please sit down. I think we have something to discuss, and I have an offer to make you." Janeway held up her hand as Mandel opened her mouth. "Don't say anything yet. Hear me out.

"It appears that you left *Voyager* with the goal of returning here to remain with this computer personality. Is that true?"

Daphne Mandel nodded.

"Can you tell me why?"

And then Mandel exploded, words pouring out over each other in a rapid rush. "When I was here and I had that link, that was like nothing you can imagine. I could see, I could think in a way I never understood before. I could use his memory, his speed, his data. I never knew it could be like that.

So wild, so beautiful. I had to come back. I had to have it forever. I can't live knowing what that feels like and not being able to touch it. To have all that power, all that knowledge . . .

"And he needs me. I can help him. The mind is so great, but the personality is so young. He trusts me. He likes me. He wants me to stay, he'll help me. No one has ever really liked me before. No one on *Voyager* will be sorry to see me go. No one in the Alpha Quadrant really wants me back. He's the only being I've ever met that really wants me."

Janeway looked at the younger woman and nodded. *Such a waste,* she thought. Mandel was so gifted. But something had happened to her personality at some point that made her unable to relate to most people.

She was truly sorry. It was all wrong. Someone with Daphne Mandel's talents should not be so isolated.

But she was not a counselor. She was captain of a starship. And she had a solution that would suit them all.

She spoke very slowly, deliberately, weighing each of her words before she said them aloud. "Ensign Daphne Mandel, do you have any desire to nurture and teach this artificial personality so that it learns a respect for living sentient creatures?"

Mandel blinked in surprise. "Of course. That's only normal. He just doesn't know better now, but I know, I know I could teach him. He hasn't attacked you, hasn't tried to reinvade *Voyager*'s systems again because I asked him not to. I told him that I was coming back and so that wasn't a reasonable option."

The captain smiled. "You do know that it was the flour that made you capable of telepathic communication?"

Daphne nodded vigorously. "Of course. I got The Doctor to tell me all about his research. He's so enthusiastic. In fact, he is something of my role model for the computer. A complete entity that is intelligent, capable but also interested in contributing to the general population.

"So it was like a gift when I found the flour in the shuttlebay. That was when I got the idea of coming back. The flour was already there. And I knew that there was power for the replicator, so I'd have plenty of food. And inside, when he does regulate the life-support, there is plenty of air and energy and heat. So I'd be able to live here indefinitely."

She was expanding on her plan like a schoolgirl who is proud of having thought of everything.

It was right, Janeway acknowledged to herself as she listened to all of Daphne Mandel's plans. This was the best option for all of them, and it would protect the region besides, end the ongoing trapping of ships for an AI's amusement. Maybe someday it would even contribute more.

Kathryn Janeway stood at formal attention, a somewhat difficult feat in the tiny shuttle. "Ensign Daphne Mandel, I hereby transfer your duty from *Voyager* to Federation Ambassador to this entity.

Let the record show that you have been honorably assigned to prevent further attacks against sentient spacefaring peoples and to one day bring this AI, and perhaps its builders, into greater participation with all the peoples of our galaxy. Congratulations, Ambassador."

The captain stepped forward and gave Mandel a formal handshake. Tom Paris followed with a salute and called her Ambassador Mandel.

"Mr. Paris, transport the ambassador and her belongings to her new quarters. And then, let's go home."